Her Ride or Die Cowboy

Texas Knights, Volume 2

Janalyn Knight

Published by Janalyn Knight, 2021.

Chapter One

Now that was some nice cowboy booty. Dallas Royle was usually too busy to notice the patrons of the Last Cowboy Standing dance hall unless they were lined up in front of her ordering drinks, but the handsome man walking by was a treat for her eyes as she leaned on the bar during an unusual lull.

Ignoring the pounding beat of the crazy-loud Red Dirt country coming from the stage, she watched him return to the small table he shared with two other cowboys. He chose a chair pointing in her direction. His face, with its strong, square jaw and high cheekbones, was as sexy as his backside. He was a handsome devil, that was for sure.

She rubbed the back of her neck and grabbed a wet towel, sweeping it across the slab of polished mesquite that made up the bar top. Her three-year-old daughter needed her mother focused on the right priorities, and a man was definitely not one of them. Piper had run a fever all day, coughing along with swiping at a runny nose. Pulling her phone out of her back pocket, Dallas checked the time. Forty-five minutes until her break.

She glanced at the dance floor, its polished wood a perfect surface for the fast-paced boot scootin' that went along with the rowdy songs the band usually played. A slow tune wafted through the air now, though. Cowboys held their girls close, swaying in a gentle two-step. Remembering what that felt like, she quickly shifted her gaze, then knelt to straighten some napkins and boxes under the bar. What was wrong with her tonight? Had she thrown her brain in the blender when she

1

made that last frozen margarita? She had a plan for her life, and she was sticking to it.

The rare respite ended, and three people at once appeared at the bar. Straining to hear their orders over the new, much louder song, Dallas flitted from one to the other, efficiently handing out beers, mixing drinks, and making change. Other customers replaced them until she found herself face-to-face with the handsome cowboy.

He smiled and handed her a five-dollar bill, almost shouting, "Bud Light, please, ma'am. Keep the change."

Dallas pulled his longneck out of the ice, popped the top off, and turned back to the man at the bar. As she returned his smile, she took in more details of his appearance. Amber eyes sparked with self-confidence. A sturdy, working-man's hand received the bottle she offered. His strong arms and broad shoulders stretched the material of his shirt. No doubt he could manhandle a 300-pound calf to the ground.

Raising the beer in salute, he said, "Thank you, ma'am," and turned away.

She had no time to watch him and his fine rear end walk away. Customers vied for her attention non-stop until a familiar face showed up. This cowboy had his arm slung over the shoulder of a young woman. Dallas frowned in surprise. Nearly every week the man came up to her bar with someone new, but last time he'd arrived with a girl wearing his engagement ring. How proud she'd been, even showing Dallas, saying the guy had just given her the sparkling solitaire. Now the jerk was standing here with a different woman. Gut-sick, Dallas scowled at the asshole as the loud pounding music beat at her senses. She spun away, shoving her hair behind her ear. *Let him wait for his beer.* Moving down to the other end of the bar, she waited on the next customer. Men were such bastards. The words *loyal* and *man* should never be part of the same sentence.

Sometimes she desperately wanted to quit working at the bar, but all she had to do was remember how badly she needed the money so that she could return to college. Supporting Piper in the way that she deserved had to be her first priority.

A few minutes later, still ready to spit nails, Dallas nodded to the waitress who came to cover the bar for her break. Grabbing her phone and car keys, Dallas strode out of the saloon-style front doors into the parking lot. As always, her car sat in the back, so she turned the corner into the deepening darkness on the side of the building. She hurried past the trucks parked on her right, focused on her car ahead at the end.

A step from her car door, she heard gravel crunching behind her. She grabbed for the door handle as a tall, heavyset cowboy clutched her arm. Yanking back, she tried to free herself, but he gripped her tightly.

"Hey there, pretty thing."

His slurred, drunken voice sent chills through her. Far from the front lot where others might hear her yell, she had no hope of help.

"Let go of me!" She jerked hard on her arm again. "Leave me alone, you creep!" She aimed a kick at his groin.

Suddenly the drunk's head smashed sideways into the top of her car. The good-looking cowboy's punch had landed perfectly, and he shoved the other man to the ground. "Go sleep it off in your truck before I call the police."

The drunk got up. He staggered to a Ford dually pickup parked a few vehicles down the lot and got in.

Dallas rubbed her arm where the man had held her and stared at the cowboy. "Were you following me?" Still angry at the unfaithful cretin at the bar, she knew she wasn't coming off as thankful as she should be.

"Nope. I'm parked over there too. I was out here getting some fresh air when that bozo grabbed you. Figured you needed help."

"Oh." What a relief. He didn't seem like a stalker, either. "Well, thanks. Wish employees didn't have to park all the way back here." Reluctantly, she reached out her hand. "My name's Dallas, by the way."

"Cash Powers. Pleased to meet you." His clasp was strong but gentle.

"I need to call my mom. That's why I came out here. My daughter's been sick, and I'm worried about her. So..." She glanced at her car door and back. "Thanks again."

Tipping his hat, he backed up a step, then turned around and walked toward the front of the building.

Dallas narrowed her eyes. He was so darn good to look at, but that didn't matter. Experience had proved that her decision to keep men at a long arm's length was the right one. Sliding into the seat, she locked all the doors before dialing her mother's number.

* * *

At two thirty in the morning, Cash drove his totally hammered friends, Jesse and Boone, through the darkness. He'd known before they'd left home that he'd be the one making sure they all got safely back to Howelton, so he'd drunk very little at the club.

Boone had turned thirty-three that day and had figured it was a great idea to get roaring drunk. Obviously, Jesse had agreed with him. They'd both given Cash hell all night because he didn't dance and hunt up women the way they did. That just wasn't Cash's style anymore. He'd learned the hard way that party girls didn't make good wives. Misty, his ex, had made him miserable before they divorced. That was a mistake he wouldn't make again.

Cash reached over and shoved Jesse, who was slumped in the passenger seat. His friends frequented The Last Cowboy and should know something about the employees. Especially the pretty ones. "Hey, you know anything about that girl bartending tonight over by the front door? Blond hair and blue eyes?"

Jesse picked his head up and stared blearily at Cash. "Yeah... Dallas. Don't get your hopes up. She don't date guys from the club. Word is she's got a kid. What I hear, she only works weekends." He leaned his head into the side window and closed his eyes.

Cash pursed his lips. What Jesse said made sense. While she waited on customers, Dallas smiled but didn't flirt like a lot of bartenders did.

It had been a long time since a woman had caught his attention. After his divorce, he'd kind of lost interest in dating. He'd tried so hard to make his marriage work, despite the fact that he'd known before their first anniversary that Misty was the wrong woman for him. The things that had first attracted him to her in college had turned into major problems when she became his wife. Accepting full responsibility for his poor choice, he'd done everything in his power to be a good husband. Her long absences from home, however, and, finally, the knowledge that she was sleeping around, had ended their marriage after four long years.

There was something about Dallas, though. It could be her fresh, girl-next-door looks, or her genuine smile, or maybe it was the confidence in the way she moved and talked. Somehow, she was different. He wanted to find out more about her. She didn't date guys from the club? He smiled. He'd see about that.

* * *

Ethan Keys strode toward the break room, eager for his first cup of coffee. His $850 Brunopasso Espresso machine had heaved its last splat of coffee this morning. He frowned. Could he stomach break-room coffee now? Women's voices carried down the hall. One of them sounded like Dallas.

A few steps from the door, he overheard her say, "One punch, and he knocked him silly. Then he threw him on the ground. Thank God he was there. I've never been so scared in my life."

Mandy, one of the paralegals, nearly swooned as Ethan walked in.

"A handsome cowboy came to your rescue. Wow! It's like the movies."

What? A cowboy had rescued Dallas? Hold on there. He'd had his eye on Dallas for ages. No way was some cowboy horning in on his turf.

"Hi, ladies. What's up?" He moved over to the coffeepot and sighed sadly as he filled his mug with something very different from what his Brunopasso made him.

Mandy put her arm around Dallas. "The most handsome man in The Last Cowboy Standing rescued this damsel in distress Saturday night." She went on to give him all the details.

Ethan frowned. "Were you hurt? That sounds awful."

Dallas shook her head and rubbed her arm. "Just a few bruises. Thank God Cash was outside getting some fresh air, or I don't know what would have happened."

Though thankful that someone had been there to help Dallas, Ethan didn't care one bit for the excitement in her eyes when she talked about this Cash guy. Working so closely with her for the past three years had given Ethan a proprietary feeling about Dallas. Dammit, he needed to do something about this cowboy business.

If the coffee was as bad as he thought, it would need lots of help to be palatable. He took his time adding cream and sugar to it.

Mandy started back to her desk.

When Dallas followed, he called to her. "Dallas, do you have a second?"

She turned around and smiled. "Sure, but just a sec. I need to get to my desk."

"How about we go out to dinner this week? Maybe make this bad memory go away. Does Wednesday work for you?"

Dallas touched his sleeve. "Oh, thank you for inviting me, Ethan, but Piper was sick all weekend, and she's still on the mend. I need to stay home."

Damn and double damn. He forced an understanding smile and nodded. "Children need their moms when they're not feeling well. Sometime soon, then, okay?" It had been a year since he'd asked her out last. Back then, Dallas had said that at two years old, her daughter was going through a stage where she got upset when her mother left her. So he'd waited all this time to ask her out again. No way would he lose her now to a freaking cowboy.

She nodded. "Sure, Ethan, and thanks again for thinking of me."

He chewed his lip as she walked out the door. With that handsome cowboy on the horizon, he had to step up his game.

He wasn't sure what it was about Dallas that made him so crazy for her. For years he'd watched her at the firm before he'd decided to ask her out. At thirty-five, he knew she was younger—in her mid to late twenties. It had been a long time since he'd dated anyone that young. In fact, in the past few years he'd dated older, wealthy socialites whom he met at the functions he attended through work. Occasionally his mother introduced him to someone in their social set in Dallas as well.

Though he enjoyed their company, Dallas was different—refreshing. She was honest and open. He loved her laugh and that she'd say just about anything. Dallas was beautiful without using a lot of makeup, and he was sure that she was a natural blonde.

She was smart—way too smart to work as an administrative assistant for the rest of her life. One of her team's paralegals had been out on maternity leave recently, and Dallas had shown herself to be so adept at research that one of her bosses, Ethan's business partner, had encouraged her to return to school and become a paralegal herself.

Ethan didn't like her working in that honky-tonk, though. She'd told him that the job funded her school savings, while her work here paid for her living expenses.

As a full partner in the firm, Ethan did very well. He couldn't help but think that if it worked out between them, he could make Dallas's life much easier. She wouldn't have to worry about money, and he would help with her school. He wondered if she ever thought about him in that way. Maybe it was time to drop some hints—make sure she did. After all, he could offer her so much more than any cowboy could.

* * *

The following Friday night, Cash parked in an empty spot near the back of the lot at The Last Cowboy Standing. He sighed out a loud gust of air. This was a first for him. Two weekends in a row at a honky-tonk? And by himself?

He took the note out of his shirt pocket, reading it for the tenth time. When he'd finished, he sighed. It would have to do. Refolding the paper, he shoved it back in his pocket and opened his door. He couldn't believe the way his heart was pounding. How long had it been since he was nervous about a woman? Ages, that was for sure. He clenched his hands to hold them steady. After the huge mistake he'd made choosing a wife, he had no confidence in his taste in women. *I hope I did a better job this time.* Beeping the locks on his truck, he squared his shoulders and strode toward the entrance.

It was nine o'clock, and the place was just beginning to roll. The band was hammering out the tune of a rowdy North Texas Red Dirt country song, and dancers were twirling around the floor. Dallas's bar was busy. Standing back, he waited his turn.

As he stepped up to order his beer, Dallas looked at him, eyes wide with surprise. "Cash. You're back."

He smiled. "Yep, I am. How are you?"

"Fine. Um, thanks again about last Saturday night. I really appreciate it."

"You're welcome. Glad I was there to help." He nodded. "Bud Light, please."

When she brought his beer, he handed her a five with his note folded inside it. "Keep the change."

She took the bill and note, a crease between her brows. "Thanks, Cash."

He found a seat not far from the bar, from where he was able to keep an eye on Dallas. Without knowing where she lived or worked, he didn't know what else he could do. The woman was busy as hell in here. Her break was the only time she could talk to him, but he wondered if she called in about her daughter during that time. He didn't want to interfere with that. So the note had been his best idea. It had to work.

* * *

The firm edges of the folded paper poked through Dallas's pocket, reminding her that she couldn't just forget that handsome Cash had come back to the club again tonight. What could he want? The bar had been too busy for her to take the time to read his note. She glanced over at his table. He was still there, watching the dancers out on the floor. Before she could turn away, his gaze swung to her and he grinned. Pressing her lips together, she smiled uneasily, though her heart thudded in response.

A short time later, a pause between customers allowed her to pull the paper out of her pocket and scan it. She felt dizzy as the blood left her face. With trembling fingers, she refolded the note and slipped it back into her pocket. Looking up, and without meaning to, her eyes met Cash's steady gaze. God, he'd watched her read it.

Heat rushed back to her cheeks and she spun around, grabbing a towel and drying the glasses the barback had washed earlier. Cash had asked her out to dinner. The worst thing about it? That flash of joy she'd felt before the stab of fear that had her hands shaking. He was the first man to truly tempt her in the past three years.

Thank God she could practically tend bar with her eyes closed. Her mind flew back to Saturday morning, when she'd taken Piper to the grocery store. She'd paused as she'd noticed a man and woman shopping together, each knowing their role, reading the list or taking items from the shelves, and calling the other *honey*. She'd blinked back tears as she passed their cart.

Dallas laid down the towel and opened a bottle of cold water, remembering Tuesday night when, after she'd put Piper to sleep, she'd caught an old rerun of *Pretty Woman*. She'd sobbed out loud at the sappy ending. That night, late as it was, she'd called Sarah, hoping for a clue to her craziness.

Sarah's answer had been as disturbing as Dallas's behavior. She'd said that Dallas should find a man who would give her unconditional love. She'd been scared ever since. Open her heart? Trust a man? Sarah was the crazy one. Yet, a tiny voice inside Dallas had agreed.

While the bar got busy again, Dallas searched her heart for an answer. Letting go of her fear of being hurt didn't feel possible. How did a person just stop being afraid? Start trusting? The only trustworthy man she could think of was her father. He was old-school. Young men didn't seem to have the same capacity. She glanced over at Cash as she handed a woman her beer. Damn. He was looking her way again. Smiling tentatively, she turned to the next person at the bar.

Later, she pulled her phone from her pocket and checked the time. It was getting late, and she was no closer to making a decision than she had been when she'd first read his note.

The pace slowed at around one thirty. She had to decide. Cash didn't dance, and, throughout the evening, he'd bought his beers at the other bar, giving her time to think. She appreciated the consideration, another clue that he was a gentleman.

Admittedly, something had been missing in her life for a while. Much as she hated it, Sarah might have hit it on the head. Maybe that tiny part of her that liked Cash's smile wanted to say yes to the dinner invitation. But, hell, what if this went wrong? Could she handle it? She'd thought the pain from Piper's father's rejection would never go away, and some days it still stabbed at her. She couldn't go through that again.

She looked at Cash's table. He was draining his beer. It was last call, and her time had run out. Ripping a piece of paper from the register, she scribbled quickly as customers headed to the bar.

* * *

The Highliner bar was packed, as per usual, as Dallas arrived during happy hour on Wednesday. She spotted her best friends, Sarah and Kate, sitting, as always, near the middle of the room, where they could keep an eye on everyone coming and going. Dallas sat down and caught the busy waitress's eye, and she swung by the table to take Dallas's drink order.

Kate leaned in. "Sarah and I had time to catch up while we were waiting for you. Tell us what's going on. All of a sudden you're leading an exciting life."

Dallas grinned. "Am not. One rescue from the clutches of death, and you think my life is exciting? Phooey."

The girls rolled their eyes and waited for her to continue.

"Well, Ethan asked me out."

Kate clapped her hands. "Yay! I was hoping he would. He's a wonderful catch for you, Dallas. He moves in all the right circles, makes great money at the firm, and you said he's really nice to you."

"He is. I had to turn him down, though. Piper's little tail was still dragging when he asked."

Kate leaned in and covered Dallas's hand with her own. "Listen, girlfriend, chances like this don't come along every day. Let me remind you how you grew up. No new shoes till your old ones rubbed blisters on your toes. You never had nice clothes like the other kids. Hardly even had enough to eat. Do you want Piper growing up like that? You're putting all your eggs in one basket, counting on finishing your legal degree. Wouldn't it be awesome to just *want* a degree, instead of desperately needing one? Promise me you're going to accept next time he asks."

Dallas swallowed and looked down at her glass of wine, turning it in circles. She still remembered her first day of third grade. One of the bigger boys, who'd always been a bully, had pointed at her old, beat-up tennis shoes with the separated sole. "You wore those things last year, loser. You're poor." Her heart still hurt for the sad little girl she'd been. She couldn't let her daughter go through that. "I know. You're right about never wanting to be poor again. That's why I'm working so hard to get my college fund together. But Ethan really is a sweet guy. Monday he even asked how Piper was feeling."

Sarah held her wine up, and they all clinked their glasses. "We're way too serious. I want to hear me some more about that good-looking cowboy."

Dallas smiled and reached into her purse. "You won't believe this, but he came back to the club Friday night. When he paid for his beer, he handed me this note." Unfolding the half-page piece of paper, she held it up.

Sarah gawked at it. "Well go ahead, crazy woman, read it."

Dallas smoothed it a little more, and then read:

Dallas,

I'm here tonight to change your mind. Word is you don't date men you meet at the bar, and I sure don't blame you. Fact is, I wouldn't date girls if I met them there, either.

But I think you and I are exceptions. I was there the night we met for my friend's birthday. I don't normally go to clubs.

I enjoyed meeting you, though I wish it had been under better circumstances.

I'd like to spend a quiet evening together somewhere, get some dinner, and learn more about you. If you're interested, just tell me.

Here's hoping,

Cash

Sarah and Kate both whooshed out, "Wow."

Sarah stared at Dallas and slapped her hand on the table. "Well?"

Dallas fidgeted in her chair. "I didn't know what to do. He seemed so kind, but I never, ever see anyone from the club. You know I don't date, either. But I knew he wouldn't leave until I answered. He came up for his last beer, and I slipped him a note." She took a sip of her wine.

Sarah shook her head, her lips jammed together. "Girl, speak now or I swear—"

Dallas giggled. "I gave him my cell number and thanked him for asking me out."

Sarah threw her arms wide. "Finally, I can't believe it. The girl makes some sense."

"So, when are you having dinner?" Kate asked.

"Tomorrow night, since Piper's feeling okay now. Speaking of my daughter... I gotta scoot. I have so little time with her, what with working and tending bar. Oh, you girls know how I feel guilty, even when I'm in the best of company."

Leaving money for her tab on the table, she kissed each of her friends.

"Get a picture of that cowboy," Sarah called, before Dallas got to the door.

Driving home, Dallas considered Kate's advice. Should she go out with Ethan? It felt weird even considering it. After being a loner for so long, it was hard to imagine that she could be the kind of woman that dressed up and went out on dates.

Yet Ethan had always been sweet to her. And he had a way of making the staff laugh when he dropped by the break room. Though he was hyper-focused with his clients, when he stopped at her desk for a chat, he was easygoing and made Dallas feel like she was the only person in the world. Perhaps if she got through the date with Cash without having a heart attack, she might accept an invitation from Ethan. Assuming he asked again. The strangeness of the situation wasn't lost on her. After swearing off men for years, she'd opened herself to the possibility of dating not one, but two of them.

The only thing she hadn't figured out with this whole dating thing was Piper. She had so little time with her daughter. How would she fit dating into her already hectic schedule?

Chapter Two

Ethan signed off his conference call and leaned back in his chair, stretching his arms over his head. Dallas's daughter should be healthy again. He didn't want to waste any more time. If that cowboy had eyes, he'd be making a move on Dallas any day.

He stood and slipped his suit jacket on, running his fingers through his short, prematurely silver hair and straightening his tie. At nine thirty in the morning, Dallas would probably be at her desk. Clearing his throat, he headed down the hallway.

She was signing for a FedEx package as he walked into the room. He waited while she handed the tablet back to the driver.

As she finished, she asked, "Help you, Ethan?"

"Nah. How's your daughter feeling?"

"Much better. Her cough is almost gone, and she hasn't had a fever in several days. Thanks for asking."

Ethan smiled. Just what he wanted to hear. "That's great news, Dallas. Does that mean you might have some time to spend with me one evening next week? I'd like to take you to dinner and a movie."

Dallas lowered her gaze and squared a stack of papers. When she looked up, she said, "Why don't we just try dinner? Both would make it late for a work night, don't you think?"

Ethan grinned. *Score!* That was better than a rejection. "Sure thing, Dallas. How about next Monday evening? May I pick you up around seven thirty?"

Dallas nodded. "Monday works just fine, Ethan. I look forward to it."

With a jaunty step to his stride, Ethan returned to his office. Wichita Falls didn't offer the culinary choices of a city like Dallas, but he enjoyed the food at McBride's Steakhouse. He called and made reservations, ensuring he and Dallas would have a small, quiet table away from the family eating area. Then he ordered a bouquet of bright flowers.

He leaned back in his chair, pressing his steepled hands to his lips. Everything had to go right Monday night. Dallas reminded him of his steady girlfriend throughout high school. Before his chaotic, traumatic college years.

Being with Dallas made him smile and gave him a sense that life was worthwhile. No way would he lose her to some cowboy who couldn't offer her the lifestyle he could. Ethan didn't mind that she already had a child. He had plenty of money to make sure the girl was well taken care of.

He drummed his fingertips on the desk. Had he beaten the cowboy to the punch? Or had the guy slipped in behind Ethan's defenses and set up a date night? Mandy might know, but how in the hell could he ask her without making it obvious he was spying on Dallas?

* * *

Thursday evening, Dallas was ready for the first of her two dates. Cash would arrive at her house soon. She pulled over to the curb and switched the car off.

"Yay, Mimi and Papa," Piper called from her car seat in the back.

"That's right. You're having a sleepover tonight. But I'll see you for breakfast in the morning, kiddo. Okay?"

Piper nodded as she fiddled with her harness.

Dallas unhooked the straps and pulled her daughter out of the car, grabbing her overnight bag.

Dallas's mom was standing on the sagging wooden porch, wrapping her sweater tightly around her. It was warm outside, but she was perpetually cold. Dallas thought it had to do with years of chronic malnutrition. Her mother had always gone without so that Dallas and her brother could eat the best of the food her mom managed to put on the table.

Dallas mounted the steps and hugged her mom. "Thanks so much for watching her. You must be tired."

Her mother reached out and caressed Piper's cheek. "Nonsense. This child is the light of my life. Come on in."

Dallas set Piper's bag on the old, worn-out sofa and moved to the recliner where her father sat, beer in hand, a cluster of empties on the end table beside him.

"Hi, Pops."

Her dad turned his head and blearily focused his eyes on her face. "Well, hi, honey." His brows drew together slowly in a frown. "Everything okay?"

She patted his arm, the horrific scars from the military helicopter crash rough under her fingers. Burns had covered more than half of his body. A back injury along with the burns he'd sustained had permanently disabled her father at the age of twenty.

Her mom had stood faithfully by his side through years of healing and decades of alcoholism. Their family had subsisted on her father's disability check. The saving grace was that her father had never turned mean as many alcoholics did.

Dallas leaned in and kissed her dad's grizzled cheek, ignoring the familiar, strong smell of beer breath.

Walking into the kitchen she found her mother pouring Piper a glass of apple juice. Knowing that finances were so limited for her parents, Dallas provided all of Piper's food. Her mother wouldn't let her pay for her daughter's daily child care, but Dallas insisted that her mother accept "pocket money," something she'd never had.

"Mom, she's had her bath and eaten dinner, so she's ready for bed any time you think is right."

Her mother gave Dallas a hug. "You go on now and have fun. We'll be fine."

As Dallas started her car, she stared at her parents' rundown little house. Her father was unable to do most repairs, and there was no money to hire someone. The roof sagged, and so little of the white paint remained that the house was nearly gray. The cracked and broken driveway resembled a patchwork quilt. The scene advertised urban poverty.

She shook her head. Never, *never* would she allow her life to be reduced to this. Finishing school and becoming an attorney would enable her to support her daughter in the lifestyle Piper needed and deserved. Nothing would stop her from accomplishing her dream.

Dallas pulled away from the curb and drove several blocks to her small house. It was kind of rundown, too, but she wanted to be near her parents, and the rent was relatively cheap. She glanced at her watch. Damn, she was cutting it close. Cash should arrive any minute.

#

The unmistakable rumble of a diesel engine came from her drive as she was putting the last-minute touches to her makeup. She rarely fidgeted, but she was as nervous as a mouse in a room full of cats. Soon, a loud knock sounded.

Rushing to the front hallway, she swung the door open. "Hi, Cash. Let me grab my purse. I'll be right with you."

She'd tried on a gazillion outfits before finally settling on a black sleeveless dress hitting halfway up her thighs and tall black heels. Her hair was pulled up at the nape of her neck, exposing her shoulders and throat. She could feel Cash's eyes on her as she strode back into the living room, and an unfamiliar shiver of excitement ran through her.

As she locked the door, he stepped back and lifted his elbow slightly, encouraging her to take it as he escorted her to his truck. Once inside, he asked, "Any ideas where you'd like to eat?"

What a relief. The dinner would be so much easier if they ate where she felt comfortable. "Anything you don't like?"

He shrugged. "I'm open to try new things."

"How about Samurai of Tokyo Steakhouse?"

Looking in his rearview mirror and pulling away from the curb, he asked, "Know how to get there?"

"Sure do. Take a left at the stop sign up there." She relaxed into the seat and even managed to tease him about the different sushi offered at the restaurant and what it was made of. The warm, spicy scent of his aftershave, along with his deft movements as he drove, had her pulse thrumming.

She pointed ahead. "See that sign there on the right? We're here."

He pulled into the parking lot and got out to open her door.

As she stepped down, she said, "I was just giving you a hard time about all the sushi. There are tons of other things to eat here, too. You'll like it."

He grinned. "I figured with steakhouse in the name I'd make out all right."

They were seated with another small party. There was a grill in the center of the tabletop where a chef would be cooking their meals in front of them.

Dallas gestured to the table. "What do you think?"

"I've heard of places like this. It'll be fun."

She took a deep breath. So far, so good. It was time to let go, relax, and be herself.

The waiter arrived to take their drink order, and they each decided on a glass of wine.

Cash asked. "Where's your daughter this evening?"

"With my parents. They're just a few blocks from me. Piper stays with them while I work."

He nodded. "She's a lucky little girl."

The waiter arrived with their wine, and they sipped quietly as they looked at their menus.

She observed Cash out of the corner of her eye as he read. His short, clean-cut hair went well with his chiseled jaw. And with that straight nose, he had obviously never lost a serious fight, a habit some cowboys couldn't seem to resist. She liked his impeccable dress—the starched shirt and Wranglers, silver studded belt, and polished boots. It all said he cared about himself, and she found that attractive.

When the waiter came back to take their order, Dallas had chosen salmon sushi and hibachi calamari. Cash ordered hibachi beef. They'd finished their wine by the time the chef arrived at the table.

Cash flagged down a waiter and asked for another glass of wine for both of them.

Dallas turned to him. "Where do you live, Cash?"

"I have a ranch outside of Howelton, in Haskell County. It's a little over an hour from here."

"So, do you raise cattle? Own horses?"

Speaking a little louder to be heard over the applause at a nearby table, he said, "I have about 500 head and three horses right now. I downsized some with this damn drought."

She nodded her understanding and took a sip of wine.

The chef dumped rice on the griddle. It hissed as he added sauce and seasonings.

Dallas smiled and continued the conversation. "So, what else is there to know about Cash Powers?"

He squinted his eyes. "Huh. Let's see, I have an older brother, Kyle, who wanted something other than a life of ranching. When my father's health changed and he could no longer ranch full-time, he insisted the place stay in the family. I got a loan and bought my brother out. My mom and dad live in town now, but Dad still helps out some. We've always gotten along."

"I'm sorry to hear about your father."

"I went to college. Got my ag degree. Haven't dated much at all since my divorce six years ago. My four years of marriage were pure hell. We didn't have children—and thank God. Kids would have been very unhappy." He shrugged. "I live a simple life. I enjoy being outdoors, taking care of the land and stock. It's hard work, but I love it."

The chef melted butter on the grill, then dumped a large bowl of vegetables into the puddle. It sizzled as the aromas of garlic and butter permeated the air.

Cash raised his glass to her. "Now, tell me all about you."

She smiled and sipped her wine. "I have an older brother, too. Jason. We never had much growing up, and he got into trouble with the law right out of high school. His court-appointed attorney really dropped the ball, and Jason went to prison for five years. That changed my life. I decided I wanted to be a lawyer and maybe prevent that from happening to another poor soul." She stared at her glass and sighed. "If only things were so simple."

Cash touched her arm. "What happened, Dallas?"

"I fell in love with a grad student my sophomore year. We moved in together, and when I was a junior, and right before the guy graduated, I got pregnant. His name isn't on the birth certificate. Piper is *my* blessing. He'll never know what he missed."

Cash reached for her hand and squeezed it. "That man was an idiot. He gave up something very precious."

Dallas looked at Cash, her eyes fierce. "And I'm not stupid. I know how to prevent pregnancy. I came down with pneumonia and was on heavy antibiotics. My birth control failed."

She grimaced and continued. "I attended school until Piper was born, then went to work as an administrative assistant at the law firm where I am now. The money I make at the club goes into my education savings account. I *will* finish my law degree. I *will* fight for people like Jason."

"Wow, Dallas. I'm impressed."

"Well, you shouldn't be. I've made my share of mistakes."

Cash reached for her hand again. "We all have. It's how we handle them that counts."

The chef was well into his routine. The fried rice was done, and he served it into bowls all around. Shrimp, beef, calamari, and lobster were crackling on the grill, and piles of vegetables were turned as they browned.

Soon they had their dinners in front of them. Cash dug in with relish.

Dallas turned to him, her brows raised questioningly.

He lifted his fork loaded with beef and vegetables. "This is really good. I'll have to tell my friends about this place."

She grinned. "I thought you'd like it. This is one of my favorite restaurants. Thanks for letting me choose tonight." She realized then that it had happened. She was relaxed—even happy. Everything had turned out all right this evening.

Later, Cash pulled up in front of Dallas's house and got out to open her door. She slid to the ground and took his arm as he escorted her to the steps.

She turned to him and smiled. "Thanks so much for dinner. I had a lot of fun."

"You're welcome. I had fun too."

She got out her keys.

He reached for her hand. "Can I see you again, Dallas?"

"Cash, I have so little time with Piper. Can I think about it?" His face fell, and she could tell he was disappointed.

Rubbing the back of his neck, he said. "You're a good mom, Dallas. The last thing you need to be worrying about is fitting me into your busy life. Let me work on that."

Chapter Three

Heads turned as Ethan and Dallas wove their way through the restaurant Monday evening. Ethan knew they were a stunning couple—him in his bespoke suit and gorgeous, blond Dallas in her striking red dress with her upswept hair. He walked a little taller knowing that every man in the room envied him.

He held her chair as Dallas settled in at their quiet table. After he sat, he perused the wine list, deciding on a Cabernet since he, for one, would be having a steak. Closing the book, he ordered a bottle as the waiter stopped beside him.

Dallas frowned slightly at his choice, but he knew she'd like it. He did.

Ethan smiled and leaned toward her. "I want to say again, you look lovely tonight. That color suits you, Dallas."

She raised her hand to her neckline, fingering the tiny locket she wore. "I like dressing up once in a while. Honestly, I'd forgotten what it was like—and now I've done it twice in less than a week." Smiling, she took a sip of water.

Ethan frowned as the bartender arrived with the bottle of wine. Dammit. He wanted to find out about Dallas's other date. Tapping his foot, he waited as the man filled their glasses and left.

Ethan took a drink of wine and leaned in. "Dallas—"

"Hi, my name is Irene, and I'll be serving you tonight."

Really? Again? He restrained himself from rolling his eyes.

The waitress laid menus in front of them.

Dallas thanked her and opened hers.

27

Ethan chewed his lower lip. How could he bring up this other date, if that's what it was? He took another sip of his wine. "Anything strike your fancy? The steak and lobster are always good here."

"How did you know I'm starving? That sounds wonderful. What are you having?"

"We'll make it two. Speaking of two, you said you've been out a couple of times this week. Care to share?"

Dallas took a sip of her wine. "It was a first date. They can be awkward, but this one was nice."

Nice? Ethan gritted his teeth. "I'm glad you enjoyed yourself." He smiled and raised his glass to her.

Straightening the fork beside her knife, she met his gaze. "Between my two jobs, I feel like Piper and I don't spend much time together. Dating takes time away from her, and I guess I didn't think that through. I don't know how going out will work for me right now, Ethan."

He reached across the table and captured her hand. "Surely there's something we can do. Let's think about it, shall we?" Breath held, he waited for her response.

She hesitated, then nodded slowly.

The waitress returned and took their orders.

Ethan regaled Dallas with funny stories from his vacations in Europe, to Aruba, and to plays in New York. She should know the kind of life she could lead if she fell in love with him. He sensed a vulnerability in her, and he had no qualms exploiting it.

They also talked about their shared passion for the Dallas Cowboys and the team's chances for the next Super Bowl.

After dinner, Ethan walked Dallas to her front door. Reaching for her hand, he said, "Don't give up on dating yet. We'll figure out something. Promise?"

Nodding, she squeezed his hand. "Thanks for a wonderful evening, Ethan. I enjoyed myself."

He stayed on the porch as she slipped inside and waited to hear the door lock before heading to his sleek, black Lexus sportscar. As he started the engine, his mind turned over the problem. He would find a way to solve it and, in doing so, he'd make sure Dallas fell for him. And only him.

* * *

Wednesday morning, Dallas stopped typing as Mandy came by the reception desk. "What's up?"

Mandy arched her back, hands on her hips, and sighed. "I'm already tired out. Wish we had a four-day work week."

"I wish. You know my bosses, though. They want me here answering phones. You might have a shot at it, though. Why don't you ask?"

"Yeah, right. I don't see it. Not with the hours I put in around here."

Dallas nodded, and smiled. "Never hurts to dream, though."

Mandy headed off. "See you at lunch."

A few minutes later, Dallas heard a text come in on her phone. Peeking in her desk drawer, she saw it was from Cash. When her morning break arrived, she picked up her coffee cup and her phone and walked to the kitchen. Curiosity had been eating at her for nearly an hour and, as soon as she sat down with her coffee, she opened the text.

Smiling, she read that Cash wanted to take her and Piper to the Railroad Museum on Saturday and then to lunch.

She tapped her finger against her lips. This certainly solved the problem of leaving Piper when she saw Cash. And Piper would love the trains. But there was something else to consider. Did she want to introduce a man into Piper's life? It would be a first. Was it the right thing to do?

She took a sip of coffee. Did Cash even like kids? Her fingers flew.

Are you experienced with kids?

Cash sent back:

I was one once. Do I need experience? I like kids just fine."

Well, he actually didn't need experience with both of them along. And he said he was glad that he hadn't had children because his marriage would have been awful for them. That was good thinking. She shook her head. What the heck.

She typed:

We'd love to go.

He shot back:

Yay! Tell me what time works for you.

She thought a second, then sent:

10:30?

That would still give her and Piper a relaxed morning.

I'll see you girls then"

Dallas laid the phone on the table. This was big. Second thoughts bombarded her. What if Piper got attached to Cash? It would make it so much harder to stop seeing him, assuming it came to that. The last thing she'd do was let Piper get hurt.

* * *

Saturday morning, Dallas answered the door to Cash's tall, powerful presence. His flashing smile reached deep into his amber eyes. She shivered, reacting to him more strongly than she ever had. Was it because she was about to allow him into her private world? Laying her hand across her pounding heart, she stepped back. "We're ready, I think. Come meet Piper."

She led him into the living room, bidding her thrumming pulse to slow. Kneeling, she held out her arms to her daughter. "Come say hi, Piper."

The three-year-old pulled her blanket up to her chin and stared at Cash from her perch on the couch. After running her wide-eyed gaze over him several times, she finally trotted to her mother.

Dallas picked up the child. "Cash, this is my daughter, Piper. Piper, this is my friend, Mr. Powers. Do you want to shake hands?"

Piper put out her hand. "Hi, Mr. Pah-wahs." She stumbled a little over the pronunciation.

Cash grinned, and shook her hand. "That's kind of hard to say. Why don't you call me Mr. Cash? Or, if Mom lets you, just Cash?"

Dallas smiled. "Let's stick to Mr. Cash. We're working on manners around here."

Cash drove a one-ton extended-cab truck, so there was a bench seat in the back to buckle in Piper's car seat. He opened the back door on his side and helped Dallas get Piper settled in.

While he drove, Cash looked in his rearview mirror. "Have you ever been to the Railroad Museum, Piper?"

Shaking her head, she answered, "No-o-o-o-o."

"You can climb into all sorts of train cars. There are old trains and some newer ones, too."

Dallas looked over her shoulder at Piper. "I've never been there, either, sweetheart. We'll have fun together."

Cash glanced at Dallas and grinned. "I haven't been in a long time. It's a cool place."

Dallas repositioned her purse at her feet and noticed a piece of grain stuck between the ridges of the rubber floor mat, reminding her that this was a working man's truck. It smelled of fresh air and clean leather, unlike Ethan's Lexus, which had that almost acrid new-car smell. After running her hand across the door frame, she inspected her fingers for dust and smiled. Cash had probably washed his truck before picking them up. It was nice that he would do a little thing like that to make the day special for her and Piper. She admired the cowboy's handsome profile for a moment and smiled.

She reached over and patted his forearm. "Hey, thanks for taking us out today. It means a lot to me and Piper." When he turned to her, she hoped he could read how much she cared in her gaze. "You're a good man, Cash. I'm lucky to have you in my life."

Cash smiled. "You're welcome. I think I'm the lucky guy, with two beautiful ladies to spend the day with."

When they arrived at the open-air museum, he paid their admission and led Dallas and Piper to the steam engine. "This is my favorite exhibit in the whole museum. If they still ran trains like this, I'd be an engineer."

Once inside the cab, Dallas looked around her. It still had a greasy, engine smell, though the interior was spotless. It was amazing—every little boy's dream. Glancing at Cash's enthralled expression, she could see it was a big boy's dream, too.

Cash lifted Piper so she could touch some of the knobs she couldn't reach.

As they walked to the next exhibit, the morning sun's heat beat down on them. Cash held Piper's hand, explaining the purpose of the dining car and how people had been served in the old days. He led Piper through the museum, lifting her to see things and helping her climb into the cars.

Piper had all but forgotten her mother was along, only glancing occasionally in Dallas's direction. Dallas's heart twisted. This is what her daughter's life should have been like. She should have had a father to pamper her and take her places, carry her around and love on her. That bastard Dallas had fallen in love with had wanted nothing to do with the baby he'd fathered. Piper was so much better off without him. Cash, however, was a natural with kids. Piper was hooked.

By twelve thirty, after seeing all a three-year-old could handle, Piper requested that *Mr. Cash* hold her.

He grinned and opened his arms, kneeling to pick her up.

Watching Piper cuddling into his embrace, Dallas's heart melted. Cash looked as happy as her daughter did.

Patting Piper's back, Cash turned to Dallas. "So, where to for lunch, Mom?"

She grimaced apologetically. "McDonald's? The playscape will keep her entertained for a while, and we can visit a little." He'd been so awesome with Piper today, she hated to subject him to fast food. But her daughter was tired, and it was close to her naptime. In a sit-down restaurant, she might get fussy.

Cash nodded. "I'd like that."

She breathed a sigh of relief. He really was a sweet guy.

The McDonald's was nearby, and they sat inside at the playscape. Piper ate her chicken nuggets quickly so that she could join the other kids her age already playing.

Dallas leaned back in her chair as Piper slid her shoes into the bin under the slide. "Ah, a mother's dream—fifteen minutes of quiet."

Cash grinned. "Kids are a lot of work. But I get how they're worth every bit of it. Piper's wonderful."

Dallas took in the sight of him, slouched comfortably in his chair, wide shoulders relaxed, hands in his pockets as he eyed the kids scooting from one cube to the next. The gleam of curiosity and interest in his eyes matched the lopsided grin on his face. He did like children. Her heart filled with warmth. She'd been right to introduce him to Piper.

Leaning toward him, she said, "Thanks for today. I hadn't thought of something like this as a solution when we talked before." Her pulse sped up as she picked up the scent of his oh-so-male cologne.

"I enjoyed myself. We'll have to do more of it. But I'd like a grownups' night once in a while, too."

She watched the kids for a few seconds. She and Piper would be having fun together, just with company, and occasionally Piper could stay with her grandparents. It sounded like a perfect solution.

"That would be wonderful, Cash. You know, I went out twice last week after not dating in years, and I've been feeling kind of guilty. I'm glad you figured this out. I feel so much better about trying to have a life of my own."

He raised his brows, looking a little confused, then he smiled. "It was easy. I like kids. This was the obvious answer, as long as you were willing."

Piper came jogging up to the table. "Mr. Cash, can I have an ice-cream cone?"

Dallas grinned. Since when had she become second choice in Piper's attentions?

Cash patted her back. "That's up to your mom."

"Sure, but you need to sit at the table to eat it."

He stood. "Be right back."

Piper sat in her chair and watched Cash through the windows. "He's big, huh, Momma?"

"Yep, he's a big guy alright. Do you like him?"

"Uh-huh. He's my friend."

"Good. I like him too." Maybe this dating thing would work out after all. Cash was certainly worth a try.

* * *

That night, after Piper was fast asleep, Dallas sat curled on her couch sipping a glass of wine. Running her hand over the soft cushion, she remembered how proud she was when she'd first brought it home. The IKEA store in Dallas had been her go-to place when she'd first furnished her house. A barback from the club owned a truck, and they'd made several trips over the first six months that she'd lived here. He'd even helped her put it all together. She'd promised herself that not one stick of used, hand-me-down furniture would be in her daughter's world, and she'd kept that promise.

She took another sip of wine. Despite how sure she had been that she'd done the right thing by going out with Cash today, her misgivings were back. For years she'd kept on track to make her dream come true by staying at home and working hard. Would the newest changes in her life eventually derail her plans? Standing, she began to pace the minimally furnished room. That couldn't happen. She wouldn't let it. She had to be strong—committed to her goal of finishing her law degree and helping people in need. Cash and Ethan had to understand that, or she'd cut them out of her life.

Chapter Four

At five on Wednesday afternoon, Ethan stopped by Dallas's desk as she prepared to leave. "Can I walk you to your car? I need to talk to you for a minute."

Dallas smiled. "Sure. Come on."

He placed his hand on the small of her back and followed her outside. "I think I came up with a solution to our problem. A friend of mine uses a nanny service when he and his wife go out. He said that the employees have all been given thorough background checks, and that he and his wife have been very happy with the nannies that have cared for their children."

As they approached her car, he continued. "I thought it might be nice to hire a nanny to take Piper to do something fun when we have a date. Then the nanny can take her back to your parents' house for bedtime or stay at your house until you get home. I can even see if we can manage the same nanny as often as possible. What do you think?" He studied her expression, hoping for a clue to her thoughts. He'd figured it all out perfectly. She had to go for this.

Dallas furrowed her brows. "Wow, that's not something I've ever considered. Piper's never stayed with anyone but my parents. I'm not sure how she'll do. Maybe if I could meet the nanny first? I don't know. Let me think about it? But thank you so much for coming up with the idea. It means a lot to me that you're willing to do something like this for Piper and me."

Much better than a no. He clasped her hands. "I'm glad you're considering my idea. I can't stand the thought of not seeing you again." Looking into her eyes, he hoped she could see how much he wanted her.

She squeezed his hands and smiled before turning and unlocking her car door.

Ethan stared as Dallas drove out of the parking lot, a hollow spot growing in his chest. She'd gotten to him. He'd work this thing as hard as he had to. That girl was his.

* * *

Friday evening, Cash sat in his recliner, frowning at his phone. He'd spoken with Dallas during the week, but a call wasn't what he needed right now. He wanted to be with her. He missed her smile, the sweet sound of her voice, and the music of her easy laughter. He'd enjoyed spending last Saturday with her, but tomorrow he'd be busy castrating calves. His part-time ranch hand, as well as Ward Ramsey, a good friend of his who lived on a neighboring ranch, would be helping him with the chore.

Something else had been on his mind, too. He couldn't help wondering if Dallas was dating someone else. She'd said she'd been out twice. True, it could be with girlfriends, but it bothered him some. Though he knew it was none of his business, he didn't like the idea of her seeing another man. It would be awkward, but he wanted to ask her about it.

He glanced at the time. Nine. Piper should be asleep by now. Tapping Dallas's name in his contacts list, he waited for her voice.

"Cash. How are you?"

"I'm kind of bummed. I want to see you tomorrow, but I need to cut a bunch of bull calves I spent all week rounding up."

"Cut?"

"Sorry. Castrate them."

"Oh...wow. I never thought about that, I guess. Hey, we'll miss you, too. But I could use the time to do some things around the house. I'm way behind. If you're not too tired, you're welcome to come by for a glass of wine Sunday afternoon."

"That sounds great. I know Sundays are reserved for you and Piper."

"We'll make an exception. After all, you gave up your Saturday for us."

Cash scrunched his forehead, hoping for inspiration. Nothing came. "Uh, I'm not sure how to bring this up, so I'll just ask. Are you dating someone else?"

"Well," she said on a sigh, "it all kind of happened at once. He's a man I've worked with for several years, and he asked me out at the same time you did. I said yes to you both without thinking the whole dating thing through—the time away from Piper, any of it."

She continued, her voice gentle and earnest. "Cash, I like both of you. I told him the same thing about spending time away from Piper. I really don't know where all this is going. This is all new to me, and Piper has to remain my priority. Her and my goal of returning to school. I hope you'll understand."

Her honesty went a long way toward reassuring Cash. He could handle a little competition. It's not like they had a commitment or anything. Still, he couldn't help but be a little disappointed. He wanted this beautiful woman all to himself. What man wouldn't?

* * *

Dallas fluffed her hair and adjusted her bangs as she walked to the door at two thirty Sunday afternoon. Cash had called earlier and said that he was on his way. Her heart beat faster as she anticipated seeing him again. Looking through the peephole, she confirmed that the tall, handsome cowboy was her visitor.

She opened the door, and Cash smiled, holding up a bottle of wine. "Thought I'd contribute to our afternoon debauchery."

Dallas laughed and took the wine from him, stepping back to allow the big man to enter. "Debauchery? Is that what we'll get up to?"

Cash chuckled and followed her to the kitchen. "One can only dream."

She showed him her bottle. "I have this Zinfandel. And I see you've brought us an Australian Shiraz. Which shall we open first?"

Cash tipped his hat to her. "Lady's choice."

"I want to taste this Shiraz." Grabbing an elaborate wine opener from the counter, she had the cork out in no time. After splashing some into each glass, she handed Cash one and held hers up. "Here's to a wonderful afternoon. And maybe a *tiny* bit of debauchery."

Cash's grin matched hers as they touched the bowls of their glasses together.

They headed out of the kitchen, and Cash laid his hand on the small of Dallas's back, encouraging her to go ahead of him through the door.

That gentle, innocent touch was so sensual she wanted to purr.

Cash sat next to her on the couch and, after taking a drink, set his wine on the table. "So, where's Piper?"

"She fell asleep not ten minutes ago. I'm lucky she still takes an afternoon nap. If you can stay a while, I'm sure she'll want to see you."

Cash smiled and took off his hat, laying it on the coffee table upside down. "I don't have any place I need to be. I'd love to see her again too." He leaned back and crossed his ankle over his knee, sliding an arm over the back of the couch.

As he got comfortable, his dress shirt stretched across the muscles in his arms and broad shoulders, and the jeans he wore were tight in all the right places. Her breathing quickened. The more time she spent with Cash, the more strongly her body responded to him. Looking into his eyes, though, she knew it was more than that. Kindness shone through his gaze. And his smile was easy and gentle. He was a decent man, not just a handsome one.

She drank her wine and asked, "How did the castrating go yesterday?"

He blew out a breath. "It went pretty well, I guess. I don't work my cow-calf pairs too often, so the mommas are kind of jumpy. And they sure don't like being separated from their babies. With three of us, it makes the job a pretty smooth operation, though. We gave the calves shots, wormed them, and tagged and castrated them, so it was more than a slash and dash. But, since I already had them penned in the corrals, we were able to finish."

Nodding, she smiled. "It sounds like it'd be cool to watch. Like the Old West."

"Hey, you and Piper should come out to the ranch sometime. We can ride, do anything that strikes your fancy."

Her eyes widened. "Uh, I don't know about me riding, but I'll bet Piper would love you to lead her around on horseback."

He grinned. "Come on, I can teach you. I have a real gentle horse that you'll like. Don't let his name—Rambo—deceive you. He's a babysitter when he's not chasing cattle."

His charismatic smile encouraged her, and she nodded. "Okay, I'll think about it. Going to the ranch might be fun." His grinning response sent tingles to her belly, and she'd leaned toward him before she realized it.

Growing serious, he reached for her hand, drawing her next to him and settling his arm around her.

Neither said anything for a few moments.

He pulled her closer still and said quietly, "You feel good. I've wanted to hold you for a while." He picked up his glass and took a swallow of wine, sighing deeply and truly relaxing.

Her body was warm, intensely sensitive to his hard body against her. His scent, woodsy and light, filled her head.

Kissing her temple, he took another drink.

She nestled her head a little closer. "I love the chance to relax during Piper's naptime. This is the only time I have to myself." Sighing, she said, "You feel good too."

He caressed her arm and drank some more.

Dallas cradled her wineglass and closed her eyes. She felt comfortable with Cash, like she could let down her guard and be herself. His sincerity drew her in. When she was with him, he fully tuned into her. She breathed in and sighed it out, relaxing her whole body. Hopefully Piper would take a long nap. This was wonderful.

Cash gently squeezed her arm. "So many sighs. Everything okay?"

"You caught me. I was enjoying this and hoping my daughter stayed asleep for a long time. Does that make me a bad mom?" She grinned up at him.

Laughing, he said, "I don't think so. At least, if it does, then I'm a bad guy, too, because I was just thinking the same thing."

Still grinning, Dallas got up. She needed some old-fashioned country music—love ballads that made you want to swoon or cry. She opened Pandora on her phone and made sure Bluetooth was activated, then chose her favorite country station, which was always her go-to for Sunday afternoons. Music swirled softly around the room. She sat back down on the couch and slid in close to Cash.

He wrapped his arm around her again. "That's more like it. They don't make them like they used to. Don't get me wrong, I like the new stuff for partying and dancing, but for listening, you can't beat the classics."

She smiled and held up her hand for a high five.

Cash clasped her fingers and pulled her into him, bending his head to her.

Dallas watched his half-lowered eyes as his face drew near. Her heart ticked faster, anticipating the touch of his mouth on hers.

His kiss was everything she'd hoped for. A gentle brush, then his lips moving tenderly across her jaw. Heat swept through her. She wanted him at the sweet spot behind her ear, which he found, caressing it before returning to her mouth. She was hot and shivery at the same time. Her clothes felt too tight. She returned his kiss, liking the firm contours of his lips stroking hers.

Pulling back, he looked into her eyes as if to gauge her reaction.

Feeling drugged, she managed a shaky laugh. "Um, wow. That was..."

He grinned. "Yeah, it was."

Piper's voice came from the hallway, "Hi, Mr. Cash."

Dallas scrunched up her face. "So much for wishes." She stood and walked toward her daughter, holding out her arms. "You didn't sleep very long. Are you sure you're ready to get up?"

Piper nodded and looked toward Cash, climbing into her mother's embrace. "Uh-huh. Mr. Cash, are you going to take me in your truck?"

Dallas brought Piper to the couch, and the little girl held her hands out to him.

Without hesitation, he pulled her on his lap. "Not today. I came to see you at your house."

Dallas sat silently while Cash held his own in a wandering, fanciful conversation with her daughter. How did the man do it without having children of his own? He had some mad skills in the kid department. She inserted herself into the conversation. "Piper, how about a snack? Let's go into the kitchen, and I'll find some graham crackers and milk."

When Dallas walked back into the living room, she grinned. "Well, you survived that onslaught of preschooler questions."

"She's a sweetheart. And what an imagination."

Dallas gestured toward his glass. "More wine?"

"Sure. I'll have one more. Thanks."

After she refilled both glasses, she sat down next to him. "What do you usually do on Sundays?"

"Not much. Feed the barn stock, of course. Might go to dinner at my parents' house. Rest, mostly. Sometimes I hang with a friend or two. It's my one day off a week."

"So when you spend Saturday with us, does that mean you have to work Sunday?"

"Yep. Makes no difference to me, though. One day's as good as the other. Except, once in a while, I go to church with my parents."

"Really?"

"Sure. We always went when I was growing up, but since I took over the ranch, I kind of got out of the habit."

Dallas looked down at her lap. "I keep saying I'm going to find a church for Piper and me, but somehow I never get around to it. I'm tired on Sunday mornings after working at the club Saturday nights, so I put it off."

Cash reached out and squeezed her hand. "Look, you work two jobs and raise your daughter by yourself. And she's amazing. Just don't give up on it. You'll find a way to do it at some point."

When he finished his wine, Cash stood to go. "I'm so glad you suggested I come by, Dallas."

Piper, who'd eaten her snack and returned to the living room, spoke up, "Don't go, Mr. Cash."

"I need to go feed my cows, punkin."

"Can I go? Ple-e-e-ase?"

Dallas laughed. "Not today, sweetheart. Tomorrow I have to work and you go to Mimi's house."

They both walked Cash to the front door where, after kissing Piper goodbye, he gave Dallas a chaste hug, fully aware of the three-year-old's gaze avidly taking in every detail.

As the door shut, Dallas leaned against the wall. Her house suddenly felt empty. How could that be? This was her home and she enjoyed living here. But now, with Cash's absence, it felt lonely.

Chapter Five

Dallas eased her head back on the headrest in Ethan's Lexus and breathed a sigh of relief. Piper liked the nanny, who'd arrived at their house right on time. In her interview a few days before, the young woman had shown just the right mixture of professionalism and playfulness. Her daughter was looking forward to going to MacDonald's to eat and play on the playscape.

Ethan took his eyes off the road and turned to Dallas. "I assume you've been to Lake Wichita before?"

"Sure. But not in a long while."

"We're going to a lovely spot where the sunsets are perfect. Our picnic dinner came from the 8th Street Coffee House. I hope you like it. And, of course, we have wine."

She ran her hand across the butter-soft leather of the seat. The spotless, polished interior reflected the essence of the man. She couldn't remember a time when Ethen appeared wrinkled. His short haircut didn't allow for hair to be out of place, but even if it were longer, she couldn't imagine a lock falling across his forehead. Always the epitome of perfection, Ethan was obsessive in his work, and his clients appreciated that they could depend on him. His excellent track record in court was due to his extreme preparedness. The man worked hard for his financial success.

Glancing toward her, he reached across and clasped her hand, smiling confidently.

She smiled back. How lucky was she that this man found her interesting?

Later, when he spread a blanket at the place he'd chosen at the western end of the lake, Dallas could see the attraction of the spot. Just off the hiking trail, it had both privacy and a view of the water and the distant horizon. "You're right. This is perfect." That was the thing about Ethan. He planned every detail. She settled on the blanket. The air had cooled some from the heat of the day.

Ethan nodded. "I found this place a few years ago, and I love it in the evenings." He reached into the large picnic basket. "Here, let's open this wine." He poured them both a measure and sat down next to her, raising his glass. "To good company and beautiful sunsets."

Ethan's charming smile and the intense look in his eyes made her feel like she was the only other person on the planet. He had a way of listening that made it appear as though he hung on every word. Though this skill was what drew clients to him and kept them loyal, it still made her feel important, as though she really mattered to him. His shoulder brushed hers, and she welcomed the contact. Touching her glass to his, she said, "To a lovely evening."

He motioned to the horizon. "I'm guessing we have about thirty minutes to sunset. Then another half hour of light after that. How about I set out our dinner?"

As he rummaged through the basket, drawing out one item after another, Dallas asked, "Can you tell me more about yourself? I know lots about your work, but so little of your private life. What about your family?"

He hesitated for a moment. "Well, here's a story for you. I'm an only child. My father died suddenly of a heart attack while I was attending college back east, leaving my mother devastated." He'd had little time to mourn his own tremendous loss, as his mother's needs had taken over his life. "Mother was unable to cope and withdrew into prescription drugs. Luckily, our family business weathered the storm well, due to a strong board of directors and a great interim CEO."

He raised his glass and took a slow sip of wine, a pensive expression on his face. "I left school three months after my father's death. I was my mother's best hope of finding a way through her grief. After moving home, I took charge of her medications and worked with her doctor to wean her off the drugs. I transferred to a Texas university and visited Mother regularly. We're very close now."

Dallas frowned. "Ethan, I'm so sorry. That must have been awful for you. What a wonderful thing you did for her. I'm glad your mother's better now." There was that smile of his again. It swept through her like a warm wave. She hadn't realized there was such a giving side to him. It never surfaced at work. He was always suave perfection. This new Ethan drew her like a magnet.

He nodded. "Thank you." As if needing a change of subject, he held up two sandwiches. "California chicken club or chicken salad? Your choice."

She tapped the latter. "Always my favorite."

While they ate, she answered his questions about her family. He already knew some of the reasons why she worked at the firm, and she gave him a few more details. A new warmth blossomed between them, mirrored in the colors of the sky as the sun sank low in the distance.

Ethan gathered the trash and refilled their wineglasses. He settled back down beside her, slipping his arm around her shoulders and pulling her against his chest.

She leaned her head into him and sipped her wine. True to Ethan's promise, the sunset was spectacular. Her eyes drooped, and she relaxed into him, enjoying the sensation of his body wrapped around hers. Sarah had been right. This was what she had been missing.

Caressing her arm, he leaned down and pressed his lips to her forehead.

A thrill rippled up her torso. Fire burned across the path of his fingertips. She'd never reacted to him this way. Tonight, everything was different.

Ethan set his wineglass aside and pulled hers from her grasp, placing it beside his. Supporting her, he eased her down on the blanket.

Her tummy fluttered, and her pulse beat loud in her ears. That glorious smile of his lowered until his lips brushed hers. She closed her eyes as the kiss deepened. Heat rushed through her, and she ran her hands up his back. Returning his kiss, she wondered why she'd never realized what a wonderful man he was.

Ethan pulled back and gazed into her eyes. "I knew I'd love kissing you. I've wanted to do that for so long, Dallas."

She smiled, at a loss. Until recently, she hadn't much thought of him in this way. Pushing gently against him, she sat up. "What a perfect sunset. You were right about this area. It's an amazing place for an evening picnic. I'm so glad we came."

He accepted her need to cool things off and handed over her wine. "I want to ask you something before we go. You'll probably have to think about it. We'll exhaust the date possibilities in Wichita Falls pretty fast, and I was hoping you might consider branching out. I understand your work at the dance hall funds your school. What if I were to contribute what you'd earn in a weekend to your education account if you took time off once in a while to do something special with me? We have the nanny service now, and maybe your parents can keep your daughter overnight. It wouldn't be often."

His look pleading, he continued. "We could go to the symphony in Dallas, to plays in New York, and to Cowboys games. We could stay in a hotel—separate rooms, no strings. Will you consider it?"

It sounded exciting. But immediate red flags popped into her mind. How would Piper handle that much time with a nanny? Her daughter had never been away from her for any length of time. What if there were an emergency? She was Piper's only parent. Plus, weekends were always hectic at the club. The few times she'd needed coverage it had been hard to come by. Of course, in this instance, with advance notice, it might not be so difficult to get someone to fill in.

She bit her bottom lip and nodded. "I'll think about it. It sounds like so much fun. Thanks for asking, Ethan."

When there was just enough light to make it to the car, they folded the blanket and headed back.

* * *

A couple of evenings later, Dallas opened a second bottle of wine in the kitchen. Sarah had just arrived, and Kate was due any second. Thank goodness Piper had been asleep since eight o'clock.

As she poured a glass of wine, Kate knocked at the door. Dallas answered and gave her friend a hug. "Come in, come in. Sarah's in the back. I'll get another glass and meet you out there."

A few minutes later, Dallas exited the back door and walked to the area lit by candles. Her yard had no covered porch, no patio. But it had trees, and she had three inexpensive lawn chairs, each with a side table. This was a favorite spot for the three of them to sip wine and catch up on gossip. However, this time, Dallas needed advice.

As she sat down, Sarah said, "Remember Acacia from Howelton? We were best friends with her at Midwestern State? She's been engaged to a cowboy named Johnny for quite a while now, and she's getting married in a couple of months."

"How wonderful. Give her my congratulations, will you?"

Kate settled into her chair and took a drink of wine, nodding at Dallas. "So, what's up, sister? Let's hear the skinny."

She twirled her glass, searching for clarity in her thoughts. "I... Well, I don't know what I'm doing. I'm dating for the first time in years, and what the heck happens? Of course, I'm seeing two men at once! It's so confusing. I have real feelings for both of them."

She put her wine down and gestured to herself. "And this body? It rocks and rolls for both of them. How can I do that?" She drew in a deep breath and picked up her glass.

Sarah spoke up. "Well, my body revs for Ethan, too. Whose wouldn't? And your cowboy sounds amazing. That's just nature, baby."

Kate asked, "You told them both you're dating someone else, right?"

Dallas nodded. "No real specifics, but yes."

Sarah said, "Well, I don't see your problem, worrywart. You're being honest, and these guys are really into you."

Dallas grimaced. "The other night, after I kissed Ethan, I felt somehow disloyal to Cash."

Kate plopped her wineglass down. "Well, that's crap. You don't have a commitment with either guy. You're just getting to know them. It may turn out that one of them is the man of your dreams, and maybe not. But right now you're exploring. If the shoe was on the other foot, they'd do the same damn thing with you."

Sarah raised her glass. "You tell 'em, girl!"

Dallas laughed. "I love you both. You know that, don't you?"

To a chorus of *Damned straight* and *Hell yeah*, they clinked their glasses together.

Chapter Six

Cash pulled into Jesse's driveway and parked behind his truck. Jesse had said he'd be home this evening, which was surprising for a Friday night. As crazy as it sounded, Cash had actually come by for some relationship advice from his freewheeling bachelor friend.

Jesse answered the door with a cold, unopened beer in his hand. He thrust it at Cash. "Here, let's get this party started."

Cash laughed. "I'm not up for a party tonight, partner. But I'll take the beer."

Jesse walked over and slouched down on the couch, picking up his longneck. "So, what does my best bud want to talk about? You've had me guessing ever since I got your text."

Cash sat in the chair opposite. His forehead wrinkled as he considered what to say. How could he bring this up without sounding like a wimp? "Uh... I was wondering. What would you do if someone you liked—a girl—was seeing someone else? I mean, at the same time as you?" Heat rushed to his face. This was bad. He so regretted coming over.

Watching Cash's face turn red, Jesse cracked up. "We're talking about you, right? Oh, man. I never thought I'd see the day. The mighty Cash Powers is getting two-timed." Jesse slapped his thigh and chugged his beer.

Cash scowled. "Ha, ha. Very funny. Are you going to answer me, or do I walk out the door?"

Jesse quit grinning and took another gulp from his bottle. "Sorry, bud. You got to admit, though, this is kind of hilarious." He rubbed his hand across his jaw. "I wouldn't like it, I know that. I expect my women to be faithful. The question is, though, *is* she your woman?"

Cash heaved a gusty sigh. "Not really. We talk on the phone, and we've done a few things together. But I like her a lot, and her daughter's a great kid. I *want* her to be my girl."

Jesse smiled. "Wishing and being are two different things, bro. Sounds like you two are just getting to know each other. There's no commitment yet. So, no harm, no foul. Comes the time you're both ready to be exclusive, it's a whole other story."

"That's what I thought you'd say. I tell myself that, but I can't wrap my head around her going out with this other guy."

Jesse laughed. "Aw, you're just jealous. You want her all to yourself. Who wouldn't?"

Cash grinned sheepishly. "You're right. I guess I am."

"Hey, buddy, you're the better man. I haven't met this other dude, but I know you. If you step up and show this girl what you're made of, she'll choose you, hands down. I'm damn sure of that."

Cash nodded, his eyes narrowed. "I need to get over myself. She's worth fighting for. I'll make sure she chooses the best man—and that's me."

* * *

Ethan checked his reflection in the glass of his framed diploma, straightening his tie and smoothing his already perfect hair. The letters on the document swam into focus. That diploma had cost him so much—and not just the money he'd paid for school. His dad had wanted him to study business and take over as CEO when he retired. But the challenge of the courtroom had always pulled at Ethan. He couldn't imagine anything more boring than chairing the Board of Directors' meetings and managing a corporation. He wanted the contests of wills with opposing attorneys and the thrill of winning that trials could afford him.

After incredible pressure from his father, he'd agreed to become board-certified in corporate law after graduating. In the end, it didn't matter. His father had died before he could prove to him that he would be a success in his legal career. It was Ethan's greatest sorrow.

He sighed and headed down to speak with Dallas.

When he approached, she looked up and smiled.

"Hey, Dallas, you about ready for lunch?"

She glanced at the clock on her computer. "I guess it is about that time."

"Great. Can I talk to you for a few minutes? Outside?"

Locking her screen, she said, "Sure. No problem."

They chatted until they reached the shade of the trees. Ethan took his hands out of his pockets and gestured enthusiastically. "Dallas, I have this wonderful opportunity, and I hope you'll share it with me. A friend of mine gave me tickets to the Cowboys' training camp in Oxnard next week. It'll be an overnight stay, but I'll pay for the nanny for Piper—as well as everything else, of course. It'd mean so much to me if you'd come. What do you say?"

Dallas, her eyes wide and slightly out of focus, looked a little overwhelmed. "What, we'd, like, fly to California?"

He laughed. "Yes, and I checked. There's a non-stop both ways that will work for us. I'll book a car and driver. We can relax, drink wine, and have a fantastic time. I know a beautiful place to stay. I reserved a two-bedroom suite in case you're able to come."

She sucked her lower lip between her teeth. "Wow, let me think. I've never done anything like this before—gone off and left Piper. But it sounds amazing. You know how much I like the Cowboys. Can I let you know tomorrow?"

Ethan followed Dallas back inside, wanting to kick his heels in the air. The excitement in her eyes was unmistakable. He figured there was a 90 percent chance that she'd say yes. He'd make sure every detail was nailed down and show her the best time of her life. Let that cowboy match this!

* * *

The following week, Dallas clinked her wineglass with Ethan's and leaned her head back into the lush, butter-soft leather seat of the limo Ethan had rented for their two-hour ride to the airport. When she'd walked out of the office and he'd led her to the long, shining black car, her mouth had fallen open. She'd assumed that Ethan would drive to the airport and hire a car for their time in California. This was an unheard-of extravagance.

Her day had been hectic. The temp covering her desk tomorrow would do little more than answer phones, so Dallas had tried to cram two days' work into one before leaving today. All the while, she'd anxiously considered what impact her long absence would have on Piper, and whether the nanny would be the same one they'd had before, as the agency had promised. Or whether Piper would get sick while she was gone. Basically, she'd worried herself to death the whole day long.

Realizing that her forehead was scrunched, she reached up to smooth it with her palm.

Ethan frowned. "You okay? What's wrong?"

"I'm tired. Today was crazy. And I spent the day concerned about things I can't do anything about."

He gave her hand a squeeze. "Relax and enjoy yourself, Dallas. You deserve this."

He was right. Smiling, she returned the pressure of his hand. "I will. No more worries."

They arrived at the airport just in time. Ethan had booked them in first class, so they were able to board right away. As the plane rose above the city, it was as if her troubles dropped away with the ground below. First class served dinner once they were settled into their flight, and Ethan ordered wine. And, as always, he kept up an interesting conversation. She was quite relaxed by the time the pilot turned on the *Fasten seat belt* signs for landing.

While the plane taxied to the terminal, Ethan called their driver, letting him know they had landed.

As they exited the building, a town car pulled over to the curb and the driver got out, holding up a sign with Ethan's last name on it.

Ethan waved to him.

The driver was dressed in a black suit and tie. He extended his hand as he approached. "Mr. Keys?" At Ethan's nod, he continued, "I'm Killian. Let me get those bags for you." Ethan and Dallas had each only brought a carry-on to save the whole baggage-claim thing.

She relaxed as the car sped off into the night. Ethan's hand settled over hers, and she squeezed it, thankful for this wonderful experience. He led such an exciting life. How lucky she was to be included in it this time.

Ethan rubbed his thumb across hers. "What are you thinking?

She opened her eyes and stared dreamily over at him. "Nothing, really. And that's amazing. I'm just relaxed...and happy. I'm glad I came."

He tilted his head back and laughed. "I'm happy too. I can't tell you how glad I am that you're here with me, Dallas." He increased the pressure on her hand, encouraging her to slide close to him. Then he wrapped his arm around her.

Leaning her head on his shoulder, she closed her eyes again. Maybe it was the wine, but this was heaven.

When they arrived at the hotel, they agreed to meet in the suite's living area after dropping off their bags in their separate rooms.

Dallas checked her makeup in the mirror, stalling for time. Now that she'd arrived at the hotel, everything had changed. Suddenly she was aware that she and Ethan would be sleeping with just a connecting room between them. Why hadn't she thought of that before? It had seemed okay until she got here. Now it was all too intimate, too personal. What had she gotten herself into? What was he expecting? Oh, why had she drunk so much wine? Her hand shook as she applied more lipstick.

She couldn't put it off any longer. Taking a deep breath, she opened the door to the living area.

Ethan turned and smiled at her. "There you are. I wondered if you'd fallen asleep." He held out a glass of wine.

Dallas shook her head. "Oh, no, I don't care for any."

"Oh, come on. You'll like this one. I insist."

Reluctantly, she accepted the glass and took a small sip. At Ethan's inquiring gaze, she said, "It's quite good."

He smiled and led her to the dining table. "The dinner on the plane was small, so I ordered something to snack on. There are several types of cheese."

Cutting a slice, he laid it on a cracker and placed it on a napkin in front of her. All the while, he carried on a breezy conversation.

Dallas took a nibble and tuned in to Ethan. He was so easy to talk to. It was no wonder his clients liked him. The knot in her belly slowly unwound. She was being silly. This was Ethan, and he was the same kind man she'd worked with for years. Smiling, she took a sip of wine.

Ethan still looked as fresh and put together as he had when he'd arrived at work this morning. Her gaze traveled over him as he seated himself. Unlike Cash, whose muscles swelled through his clothes, Ethan's lithe, muscular body hinted at its strength in his grace of movement and the stillness he could hold when he listened to her. Her pulse beat more strongly as he turned and smiled. He was like a magnet, pulling at her.

Reaching out, Ethan brushed her hair from her temple and caressed her cheek. "You're gorgeous, Dallas. I don't think you realize how beautiful you are."

She licked her lips. Warmth swirled through her belly as Ethan rubbed his thumb across her hand, the simple caress incredibly sensual. "Thank you. I have good genes. I've seen pictures of my mom when she was young, and I look a lot like her."

He picked up the snack tray and his wine. "Let's make a move." Walking farther into the room, he placed the food on the coffee table.

A trickle of anticipation slipped through her veins as she followed Ethan's trim backside. "What time do we need to leave in the morning?"

He held out his hand to her as they settled on the couch. After pulling her in close, he answered. "Let's have breakfast here in the room and leave around eight thirty. Does that sound all right with you?"

"Sure. I can't wait to get there." At Ethan's smile, she tilted her head into his shoulder.

Ethan set his wine on the table, then did the same with hers.

Her pulse thrumming, she felt the first brush of his lips like a bolt of electricity, revving her up like a racing engine. She pulled back. She had to get a grip.

He raised his brows. "You okay?"

Biting her lip, she nodded. "Yes, sorry. This is all a little overwhelming."

Ethan smiled. "I'm still me. You're still you. We just hopped a thousand miles in the air." With a gentle smile, he squeezed her hand.

Expelling a gusty sigh, she knew he was right. "I'm being silly." She smiled. "Where were we?"

He grinned and reached for her. "Let me see if I can remember."

Dallas leaned into his kiss, in control and ready to savor his touch.

Slipping his hand into her curls, he explored every inch of her mouth with his soft kisses.

Breasts tingling, she caressed his chest and kissed him back, wanting him closer, to feel his body against hers.

He eased her down on the cushions and nibbled her neck, drawing a hissing breath from her.

Running her hands up his back, she searched for his mouth.

"Kiss me," he commanded.

Her heart pounded in response, and she complied.

He interlocked his fingers in hers and raised both arms above her head. "Harder, Dallas!"

Yearning for his lips, her pulse throbbing in her ears, she kissed him hard, nipping his lower lip.

Brushing his mouth across hers, he smiled and pulled back. "Good."

She gazed into his blue eyes, wondering what had just happened and why it had affected her so much.

Ethan raised a brow. "You okay with that?"

"Um, I'm not quite sure what *that* is."

"Does it scare you? It needn't. We're meant to enjoy it."

"It was unusual, but...nice, I think. Different. More...ravenous?" She grinned.

He laughed. "A good choice of adjectives. I feel ravenous too."

Dallas sat up. "I need some sleep. I'll be getting up early if I'm to have any breakfast before we leave."

He stopped her when she turned to go to her room. "A kiss goodnight?" He wrapped his arms around her waist and pulled her close.

The pressure of his chest hardened her nipples, bringing them intensely alive. As Ethan caressed her tongue with his, heat swept over her skin like a fever. She sucked his lip and nipped playfully before pulling away.

He moaned and slipped his hand into her hair, giving her a bruising kiss, molding her body against him in a tight embrace.

She kissed him back hard and pushed away, breathing like she'd run the 200-meter dash. "Wow."

He grinned and cradled her chin, his eyes laughing into hers. "Goodnight, Dallas."

Grinning, she said, "Ravenous? Goodnight, Ethan."

* * *

Dallas stuck her finger in her ear and pressed her phone tightly to her other. "Hello? Cash?" The sound of the Cowboys fans in the stands was too loud to hear his voice any other way.

"Dallas? What am I hearing?"

"Hi. I'm in Oxnard at the Dallas Cowboys training camp. Ethan was able to get tickets. I can't believe I'm actually here!" She adjusted her phone, pressing it tighter to her ear.

"Really?" His voice sounded strange. Hesitant.

"Yeah, we're coming back tonight. Listen, can I call you when I get back? I can hardly hear you."

"Uh, sure. And, uh, have fun, Dallas." Enthusiasm was definitely lacking in his voice. Now she worried that he was upset that she was here with Ethan. Damn, she couldn't forget to call him tomorrow.

Ethan turned and noticed that she was on the phone. He raised his brows. She shook her head and put her phone back in her purse. The crowd roared as someone scored a touchdown, and she yelled and applauded along with them. She wouldn't let anything spoil her joy in this once-in-a-lifetime experience.

Ethan slipped his arm around her shoulders and grinned down at her. She was so lucky to be here and to be with him.

* * *

The next evening, the plane dipped below the cloud layer as it descended. The lights of Dallas/Ft. Worth spread over the vast horizon in every direction. Ethan's hand comforted her during the noise and vibration caused by rapid deceleration. The runway swung across her view and disappeared.

In the limo on the return trip home, she turned to Ethan. "I'm sad this day is over. Meeting the players and watching them practice was so much fun. How can I ever thank you for this?"

He squeezed her fingers. "I'm so glad you were able to come with me. I had a wonderful time too. It was too short, though. I want to plan something soon where we don't have to rush back. Okay?"

Smiling, she said, "Let me see how Piper did. I tried not to worry about her while I was gone, but now that I'm almost home, I'm anxious to see her and find out how she managed without me."

Later, as Ethan walked her to her door, she eagerly accepted his embrace and hungry kiss before saying goodnight. Once inside, she leaned against the closed door, smiling, all thoughts of Cash chased from her head. Surely this would be the man she fell in love with.

Chapter Seven

Cash goosed the truck again, traveling too fast down the pasture road. He'd hardly slept the night before. Imagining Dallas in California with that other guy had been almost more than he could bear. Although he didn't think she was sleeping with him, the whole situation brought back feelings he'd had during his marriage to Misty, and he never wanted to go through that again.

At Jesse's house, he'd talked a big game. As though he could take a little competition. As though he knew that he was the better man. If this was what a relationship felt like, though, he didn't want it. He'd stayed away from women for years, and he should have stuck with that.

Why the hell couldn't women be happy with one man? He slammed on his brakes and slid around a curve, then jammed his foot down on the accelerator again, the truck bumping and bouncing through potholes. He clenched the steering wheel. The real question, of course, was why wasn't he enough for Dallas?

It shook him. Cussing long and hard, he pulled over into the borrow ditch so that he wouldn't wreck his truck. He wasn't the man he thought he was if he couldn't handle the situation. He lurched out of his door and leaned against the side of the truck, crossing his arms in disgust.

What he couldn't figure out was why Dallas didn't choose him, now, without question? They were getting to know each other, and he could tell she liked him—was even attracted to him. So why didn't she quit all this foolishness?

He gusted out a sigh. She was worth fighting for, but how could he hang in there when this whole thing felt so awful?

Some way up the road, a hawk dove from high above and caught a jackrabbit. He wandered over to get a closer look. By the time he got back to the truck, he'd made up his mind. He'd give Dallas more time.

* * *

Wednesday evening, Dallas settled back on the couch and sighed. This was the first time she'd been able to relax all day. Work had been extremely hectic after her two days off, and Piper had wanted her undivided attention this evening, even begging her momma to rock her to sleep. Taking a sip of wine with her eyes closed, Dallas let it slip slowly down her throat. This was heaven.

After worrying off and on all day about what to say to him, she realized it was time to call Cash. Dating two men hadn't gotten any easier. In fact, it was getting much harder. Still with no idea what to say, she grabbed her phone.

Cash answered on the second ring.

"Hey, is this a good time?"

Clearing his throat, he said, "Sure. How are you? How was your trip?"

"I'm exhausted. Taking off work is never a good idea. I'm always swamped when I come back. But the trip was fun. I never in a million years thought I'd see the Dallas Cowboys practice. I even talked with three of the players. I'll remember that forever!"

"I'm glad you had a good time, Dallas. How did Piper do with her momma gone?"

"I was worried about that. A nanny took her on a picnic at a playground for dinner and then to MacDonald's for ice cream, though she slept at my parents' house. Still, she missed me badly. I had to rock her to sleep tonight."

"Well, of course she did. You deserve time on your own, though."

Dallas ran her hand through her hair and tucked her leg under her. "Cash... I know... Well, this can't be easy for you. I'm not sure I could take it in stride if I were in your place. I'm sorry for any pain or—"

He interrupted her. "I'm dealing. I'll be honest, though. It's been a little rough. I care about you, and I want you to myself. I think anyone would in my position."

When she talked to Cash, his honesty, his goodness, all the blatant sexiness that was him, came rushing back to her. How could she have been so sure she'd choose Ethan?

"You're right. I totally get it." She wanted to reassure him in some way, but he spoke first.

"I need to see you, Dallas. Alone. I know you should spend time with Piper this weekend. Are you free Monday night?"

Sensing his urgency, she readily agreed. "Yes. What are we doing?"

"If you just throw on a pair of jeans, how soon could you be ready?"

"Uh, six fifteen?"

"I'll pick you up then."

* * *

Monday afternoon, Dallas scrambled to her parents' house to get Piper. She only had an hour to feed her, bathe her, and get her back to her mom and dad. Piper, bless her heart, got with the program and ate quickly, something she didn't always do. That allowed for a few minutes of playtime in the bathtub and for Dallas to change her clothes. Afterward, Dallas lifted her out, scrubbed her down with a towel, and slipped her into her pajamas.

By the time she backed out of her parents' driveway, it was six thirteen. She was barely going to make it.

Cash was waiting on the curb when she got home. A thrill of anticipation swept through her as she waved and parked in the drive.

He opened the truck door for her. "Was it hard for you to get ready this early?"

Grinning, she said, "Well, let's just say that I beat the speed record for getting Piper fed, bathed, and ready for bed."

"Wow. Why didn't I think about you needing to do all of that first? I'm sorry. I'm still getting the hang of figuring out Piper's needs too."

"No worries. Please tell me I won't be meeting anybody new. I look like something the cat dragged in."

He grinned. "Do not. And no, you won't. It's just me and you tonight." Reaching into the back seat, he pulled out a small, soft-sided ice chest. "I put several kinds of sodas in here and a water. That's it for now. The open-container law sucks."

She rummaged around and found a diet drink. "Fine with me. Who needs to be arrested? Want one?"

"I had one on the way to your house. So, tell me about the Cowboys training camp. Who did you meet?"

In great detail, she told him about each of the three players she'd spoken with. By the time she'd finished, she looked out the window and noticed they were on a country highway. "Well, the jeans were a hint. Now we're in the boondocks. Where are we going, cowboy?"

He laughed. "About thirty minutes farther into the boonies. My place. I want you to see where I live and work." Clasping her hand, he rested it on the console between them.

Smiling, she leaned back and sighed. "Cool. A real cattle ranch. Now I'll be able to picture what you're talking about when we're on the phone. I'm glad we started early so it won't be dark."

True to his word, a half hour later they pulled in under the sign of the Rocking P ranch.

Cash drove through to the barn and parked. "I'll show you around here before the sun goes down." After opening Dallas's door, he clasped her hand and walked her inside. He motioned to the nearest stalls. "These two are first-time heifers, due to calve in the next day or two, I guess. I'm keeping an eye on them in case they have problems." They continued down the breezeway. "The other three are from the barn pasture where I keep my granny cows. They calved in the last day or two and need some TLC. I make sure that the cow gets extra feed and that the calf is eating good before I turn them out with the others."

Dallas was fascinated with his descriptions. The animals were so calm, chewing their hay and watching everything she and Cash did. "I guess you fed before you came to pick me up?"

"Yep. Believe me, you'd hear hollering if I hadn't. They let you know if they miss a feeding." He continued the tour through the corrals and then showed her some steel hog traps, explaining that wild hogs came around the barn at night, getting into the cows' feed and tearing up the round bale stacks.

Cash led her to a green Kawasaki Mule. "Climb in. I'll show you the home pasture. I've got about sixty head there, plus a couple of nice bulls."

After he stopped, got out, and opened the first gate, she offered to be the gate man and close it.

Cash grinned. "Girl, you just made my day. Opening gates makes a rancher's life hell. I'll warn you, once you start, it's a hard job to get shed of."

She laughed. "I don't mind. I need the exercise. I sit all day at a computer." The Mule surprised her, reaching speeds of thirty-plus miles an hour on the dirt roads of the pasture. The wind in her face and Cash's nearness had her pulse pounding.

He knew all the animals' hangouts, so they were able to find almost all of the cattle, including one he was most proud of, a Black Angus herd bull.

Pulling up at one of the ponds, he turned off the engine. "Just look at that big bast—ah, bull. I paid quite a bit for him, but he's been worth it. He throws small calves, so he's a great heifer bull. His conformation is perfect. He's not mean either. I can go in and separate cows or move him into another pen without a problem."

Cash's animated face as he described his bull made her smile. It was obvious he enjoyed his work and cared about his animals. She loved getting to know this side of him and figured it was something many people didn't see. Admiring him, wanting a connection with him, she reached over and clasped his hand. "He's magnificent."

Cash grinned and wrapped his arm around her, snugging her up close. "He is, isn't he? Come on, I'll take you back and show you the house. I grew up there."

He explained that the original rock ranch house had been built by his family in 1892. Rambling additions had been added over the years and had all been remodeled at different times. A long, covered porch ran the length of the front of the house.

It was almost dark as they pulled up. Cash said, "Now the house is a monster. There are six bedrooms. Mom and Dad are counting on me to fill it with lots of tiny feet again."

Dallas laughed. "Oh, so there's no pressure or anything." Did Cash want lots of children? Did she?

"Right. Sometimes I think my brother got the better deal."

Once they were inside, Cash gave her a quick tour of the main part of the house, then she followed him back into the kitchen. "So, I guess at some point there were a lot of people in this house?"

"Yep, big families were popular back in the day. Dad kind of let Grandpa down with only two kids."

She grinned. "He went for quality rather than quantity."

Cash laughed. "I agree. Listen, everything's ready to make us a steak dinner. It'll take too long to cook them on the grill, so I'll make them in a skillet."

There was something sexy about watching Cash move around the large farm kitchen as he cooked for her. Especially when he stopped every few minutes to lean in for a kiss. This was one of the rooms that had been recently updated. Newish appliances and tons of cabinet space made it a place a person would be happy to cook for their family in.

Cash turned his head and caught her eyes focused on his butt. Grinning, he raised a brow and put the spatula down. "Come here, you." He pulled her to her feet.

A wave of desire hit her as he devoured her mouth. She slipped her arms around his neck and kissed him back, hard, wanting him to feel how much she cared about him, desired him.

With a final cheeky smack on the lips, Cash drew back. "Now that's what I call a kiss."

Breathlessly, Dallas sat, grinning. "Um, I concur, and I think I'll keep my eyes to myself from now on."

He laughed and returned to the stove.

After dinner, he opened a bottle of wine and poured them each a glass. "We need to be getting back, but not just yet, okay?"

She nodded as he led her into the family room and over to a large leather sofa.

After they settled in next to each other, he clasped her hand and turned to her. "Dallas, I could have easily invited you and Piper over here on a Saturday, but I wanted to do this tonight, alone, for a reason. I need you to understand how I live, who I am. I can't give you fancy trips to California, at least not often. It's not so much the money. I don't travel a lot because a rancher can't. There're always cattle in the barn, and they eat twice a day. And the pasture cattle need to be fed and checked on regularly. It takes planning to go on vacation when you raise livestock for a living."

He ran his gaze over her face, as if trying to gauge her reaction.

Squeezing his hand, she said, "I understand, Cash."

"If things get serious between us, Dallas, I have a lot to offer you. Once I give my heart, it's yours forever. And I'm faithful. I don't fool around. I work hard and manage my finances well. I love kids, and I want a family. Piper would be just like my own, if you'll allow it. I'll support you going to school any way you need. Of course I'll support your career. I just know that being a lawyer means you'll be crazy busy. All I ask is that you carve out regular time for your family too."

Her heart felt twice its size, filled with joy that this strong, caring man had laid himself bare to her. He was right. He had so much to offer her. Caressing his cheek, she said, "Cash—"

He covered her hand with his. "No," he interrupted her, "don't say anything—not right now. I wanted you here tonight because someday soon you'll make a decision, and I want you to make it knowing what you're choosing—or giving up."

"Can I say one thing?"

"Go ahead."

She smiled. "Will you kiss me?"

He stood and pulled her to her feet without taking his eyes from hers. Wrapping his arms around her waist, he grazed her mouth with the softest breeze of a kiss.

She moved to respond, but his mouth was gone. As she opened her eyes, he drifted another delicate kiss across her lips, creating a hot ache in her core. She stood on her tiptoes and moaned softly.

This time he taunted her with the tip of his tongue, setting her on fire.

Wrapping her arms around his neck, she pulled him down to her, taking his mouth, her lips moving hungrily over his. She wanted him. She would have him.

Cash slid his hand through her hair, slanting kisses on her lips, caressing her tongue with his. Cradling her face, he branded her with his sensuous touch.

She twined her leg around his, pulling him closer still.

Pulse pounding in her ears, she realized she had to stop. Her rampant body was taking her much further than her heart and mind were ready to go. Pulling back, she opened her eyes. Cash looked as wild as she felt. She bit her lower lip. "I'm sorry. I... Uh, I guess you can tell it's been a while since I... Since Piper's father, actually."

He took a breath and smiled down at her. "You don't need to explain anything. You were great. Really."

"No, I'm not like this. At least, I didn't used to be. I don't know what I'm like now. I haven't been with anyone in almost four years. But my body has a mind of its own. If I don't watch out, it takes off and pulls me along for the ride."

Cash grinned. "I'm aware of that one. I think men have that problem a lot."

"Well, I can't have problems like that. Not anymore. I have Piper to think of. Everything I do affects her. I can't forget that." Shaken by her lack of self-control, she stepped back a step.

He frowned. "It takes two to go there. If you want to take it slow, we'll take it slow. You just need to talk to me, okay?"

She sighed and looked down. "You must think I've lost my mind. I probably have. And, yes, let's take it slow for now, okay?"

He was smiling.

God, he was a wonderful guy. She smiled back and reached for his hand. "I had fun this afternoon. I love your ranch. Now

I'll be able to picture you here, sitting in this room, when we're on the phone at night."

Lifting her fingers to his lips, he gave them a gentle kiss.

That was a habit she was getting kind of fond of.

He led her toward the door. "Yep, this is where the action is, all right. You ready to head home?"

On the drive back, Cash held her hand in easy silence. She turned to her window and smiled. Surely he would be her ride or die cowboy, the man she fell in love with.

* * *

Thursday evening, while Dallas was shampooing Piper's hair in the bath, her phone rang. She let it go to voicemail, wondering who would call her at that time. All of her friends knew she'd be busy with her daughter.

Once she had Piper bathed and in her pajamas, Dallas looked at her missed calls, surprised to see Ethan's name. They spoke at the office several times a day, and the only other time he'd called her at home had been about the California trip. She shrugged. Settling in with Piper on the couch, she read her two bedtime stories—their usual routine.

Later, while sipping wine in the quiet living room, she phoned Ethan back.

He answered on the first ring. "Hi, Dallas. Glad you called."

"I apologize for the delay. I was busy bathing Piper when my phone rang."

He hesitated. "Sorry, I didn't think of that. I'll call later next time."

"I'm usually free by eight thirty or so. What's up?"

"My mother called this evening and said she's coming for a visit next week. I want to introduce you. In fact, Mother asked to meet you. She said she'd make dinner—she's a fabulous cook. I'm taking the afternoon off to help her. Mother loves having me in the kitchen as her sous chef. This all happens Wednesday evening. Will you please come?"

Dallas took a sip of wine and let it settle in her mouth. Meet his mother? She'd never even met Piper's father's parents, and she'd been with him almost two years. But then, look how well that had turned out. This invitation meant that Ethan had told his mom about her. *Huh.* That was kind of awesome. "I'd love to meet your mother. Dinner sounds wonderful."

"Great! I'll send a car for you so that you can enjoy wine at dinner and, as you know, the nanny service is at your disposal."

Ten minutes later, her phone rang again.

"Cash, hi. How are you?"

"Thinking about you."

A warm flush spread through her as she imagined him on the huge leather sofa, soft antique lighting lending a cozy touch. "Are you now? That's nice."

"I'm disappointed I can't be with you and Piper this weekend. I need to haul some cattle to the auction." He paused. "However, Jesse called this afternoon to ask if I wanted to go to The Last Cowboy Saturday night. I know you'll be busy as hell, but at least I'll see you."

"Wonderful, and I'll come sit at your table during my break." She never, ever did that, but Cash had proved he was worth breaking her rules for. To her surprise, she found that she was missing him. Like, *really* missing him. When had that start-ed?

"It's a date, then. Or, whatever. So, if you have a minute, tell me how you've been."

She didn't want to hang up, either. As she went through her day and asked about his, she leaned back, closing her eyes, lov-ing the sound of his deep voice. By the time he wound down, she was almost asleep.

He finished up. "So, that was my day. Nothing like yours. Things here are busy, but pretty laid back."

She opened her eyes and said groggily, "But good. It's a wonderful life."

He was quiet a while. "Well, yeah, I think so." He sighed. With a smile in his voice, he said, "You sound like you're ready to fall asleep. I'll let you go, and I'll see you Saturday."

* * *

Saturday afternoon, Dallas slammed her car door and raced for the Last Cowboy's front door. She was ten minutes late, and she was never late. Slapping open the saloon doors, she jogged to the bar. If anything, she always needed to be there early—but especially tonight. One of the top Red Dirt bands was going to be featured on stage, and the place would be packed. Now she had to scramble like hell to get set up.

Today had been a nightmare. After lunch, water had started spewing from the ice maker on the door of her refrigerator. She'd dragged it out from the wall only to find that there was no way to turn the water off. Putting in a frantic call to her dad, she'd learned that there should be a valve under her sink. By the time she'd located it, the water was an inch deep on her kitchen floor. It had taken every towel in the house to mop up.

She'd put in a huge load to wash. Hoping to add a second load before leaving for work, she'd stopped by the laundry room on her way out the door. The washer was silent, and her towels were sitting in a full tub of water. The damn washer was broken. Disgusted and ready to cry, she'd loaded Piper into the car and headed to her parents' house.

She shook her head and glanced at the stage. Of course a Red Dirt band was playing tonight. Though she loved the music, it made the crowds crazy. The beginning of a headache throbbed at her temples, and she dreaded the start of the loud music.

Where was she going to find the money to repair both of her appliances? What if her washer couldn't be fixed? Things like this brought home how hard it was to be a single parent. She had no one to turn to—nobody to help her when she had setbacks. This, like the other crises that happened to her, reinforced her intense drive to return to law school. She would *not* spend the rest of her life broke and scared. Hot tears formed behind her eyes, and she scrubbed her hand across them. Crying solved nothing.

"You okay, Dallas?"

Without turning around, she said to Jerry, her balding and slightly overweight boss. "Sure, I think I'm getting a headache, is all. I'm fine." Taking a deep breath, she slid into her routine. This job would make her dream come true, and it had to be her focus tonight.

The band started playing and the loud, pounding music pierced her ears, lancing through her head. Her headache ratcheted up.

A handsome cowboy leaned on her bar in the lull before the place got really crowded. "Hey, Dallas, why is that pretty face of yours frowning?"

"Is it? I should watch that. This headache is a beast, and the music isn't helping. How are you, Doug? Do you want a beer?"

"Sure, I'll take one. I'm much better now that I'm here with my favorite girl. What's it going to take to make you go out with me? I'm not giving up."

Dallas grinned and handed him his beer.

He held on to her hand a moment too long, and said, "Keep the change, sweetheart."

She laughed. "You're a flirt. Good thing you're harmless."

He put on a wounded look, hand over his heart. "Harmless? I beg your pardon? I'll have you know the women in Wichita Falls are all begging for my attention!"

As she turned to her next customer, she rubbed her forehead. Her headache might actually be better. Doug always perked her up on her long weekend shifts, and he was such a nice guy. She always wondered why he came in alone every week. He danced with unaccompanied women and flirted like crazy, sometimes leaving early with one woman or another. She sighed. He must not have found the right one yet.

A half hour later, the place was jammed with people, and the band was on fire, the raucous beat bouncing off the walls and splitting her head in two. And, in tune with a perfect day, they were short on waitresses. There was a constant line at her bar, and Jerry said he didn't have anyone to relieve her for a break. Just as she knew they would be, the people were rowdy. It took everything she had to keep smiling and keep moving.

She handed a cowboy his change and looked to the next customer. It was Cash. In all the mess of the day, she'd forgotten he was coming. His grin loosened the tightness in her chest, and she gave him a shaky smile.

He covered her hand where it lay on the bar. "You don't look too good. You okay?"

Shaking her head, she clasped his hand like a lifeline to a sane world. "I have a headache. Today has been terrible, and it looks like I won't get a break."

He squeezed her hand. "No sweat. I'll be here. You let me know if you need anything. I'll be watching you."

"You want a beer?"

After he left, the tight band of muscles around her head relaxed a little, knowing he was across the room. True to his word, each time she looked, he met her gaze and smiled.

Her headache pounded away. Jerry had asked one of the waitresses to finish at the bar as soon as they closed so that Dallas could head home as quickly as possible. Break time came and, though she couldn't take off, Jerry stepped behind the counter to let her head to the restroom.

As she came around the bar, she looked up at Cash and froze. A curvaceous cowgirl with gorgeous blonde hair leaned down for a kiss as she slid into his lap.

Cash turned his head and caught her shocked stare.

Dallas lurched into motion, heading to the ladies' room. Who was this woman who felt so free with Cash that she plastered a kiss on his face and plopped into his lap? Was he seeing her too? Hurt and confusion made her already pounding head feel like it would explode.

Once in the ladies' room and safely in the stall, she sat and closed her eyes, trying to make sense of what she'd seen. Then it hit her. What right did she have to be shocked or angry? She was doing the same thing to both Cash and Ethan. Was that who she was? A sick feeling overcame her, adding nausea to the nearly blinding throbbing behind her eyes. *God, help me make it through this night.*

Cash met her on the way back to her bar. "Dallas, it's not what you think."

Without meeting his eyes, she held up her hand, the pain in her heart matching the pain in her head. "No. You have every right. My head's killing me right now. I need to get back to work." She pushed past him and got behind the bar, starting with the first of the long line of customers bellied up there.

Around one forty-five, when things slowed some, Jerry came to relieve her, telling her to go on home and do something about her head. She slipped out without Cash noticing.

Lying in bed an hour later, filled with meds, a gel ice pack on her throbbing head, she was unable to sleep. Now that she'd had a dose herself, she couldn't bear what she was putting Cash and Ethan through. It wasn't fair to them. How had she ever thought it was? She didn't consider herself a cruel person, but that's exactly what this situation was. She had to stop. It wouldn't be right to choose either man since she wasn't in love.

Though she knew letting both men go now was the only right thing to do, the hollow feeling in her chest disagreed. She hadn't realized how much the two had filled her heart—with laughter, anticipation, joy. How could she bear no more nights on the couch listening to Cash's deep, sweet voice on the phone, no more cuddling on the lakeshore with Ethan? A heavy weight pressed her into the mattress. Hot tears welled under her closed lids. She had no choice. She'd break up with them tomorrow. She couldn't hurt either man anymore.

Chapter Eight

Cash looked at his watch for the hundredth time Sunday morning. Ten thirty. Surely he could phone Dallas now? He was beginning to think she wasn't going to answer when she finally picked up. "Hey, this is Cash. Well, you know that. Listen, please hear me out. Last night—"

"It's okay," Dallas interrupted. "I was going to call you, but I was waiting for my headache medication to kick in."

"Damn, your head's still hurting?"

"Yeah, my headache usually goes away after I take something, but this time it hasn't. Anyway, like I said, I need to talk to you." She paused. Not having expected his call, she hadn't found the right words yet. "After last night—"

"Dallas, you don't—"

"Cash, it's okay. Just let me speak. After last night, I realized how unfair I'm being to you and Ethan. My reaction, which was uncalled for, by the way, showed me that I'm hurting each of you by dating you both at the same time. In fact, it's cruel. That's not who I am. I have to stop seeing you two. It's the only way to make this right."

Cash was silent for a moment. "Dallas, I told you I'm dealing with this. Now, if you want to stop seeing the other guy because he can't take it, then that's up to you. But I'm okay. I care about you, and I want to see where this relationship goes."

She sighed. This might be the last time she heard Cash's voice. "Cash, I feel terrible about this." She paused. "Look, my head is killing me. I can't talk about this right now."

"Okay. Rest. Take care of yourself, Dallas. But I'm not giving up. Don't you do it, either."

Her thoughts spun as she disconnected. What if Ethan felt the same way as Cash? How could she go on seeing them, knowing how it felt to see someone she cared about with another person? Damn, she couldn't think about this now. She got up and switched out her ice pack. Thank goodness Piper was playing quietly with her toys and watching her favorite cartoon on TV. Lying back down, Dallas refused to think about either man. She closed her eyes.

"Momma, I'm hungry."

She awoke to Piper patting her arm. Dallas licked her dry lips. Lord, she'd fallen asleep. Gingerly, she sat up. Her headache was still there but much better. "Okay, hon, let's fix you some lunch."

An hour later, with her daughter down for her nap, Dallas couldn't put off calling Ethan any longer.

Her anxiety increased as his rich, cultured voice came on the line. "Dallas, how are you? It's great to hear from you."

Unsure how to approach the subject, she jumped right in. "Ethan, I realize now that I'm being unfair to you and Cash. Dating the two of you is hurtful, and I don't want to be that kind of person. The right thing to do is to stop seeing you both." She took a deep breath. "I'm so sorry for any pain that I've caused."

There was a long silence, then he said, "Dallas, I'm not sure where this is coming from. I always knew the score. I'm quite confident you'll choose me in the end. Go ahead and see the cowboy until you make your choice. Of course, I'd rather you stop dating him. But that's for you to decide. I'm tougher than you give me credit for." He laughed. "Really, Dallas, it's not a problem. If it becomes one, I'll let you know."

"Well—"

"Come on, let's talk about something else. I've gotten hold of some Broadway play tickets. Friday and Saturday night. Back Sunday. I'll donate to your school fund. It's not for a few weeks, so you'll have plenty of time to find someone to work for you at the bar, and we can figure out the nanny details. Please say you'll come?"

Some of her anxiety slipped away, replaced by the warmth his kindness always made her feel. She remembered sitting snuggled against him on the limo drive home from California, and a tiny thrill ran through her. It still surprised her sometimes that this handsome, successful man cared about her. And now a trip to New York? What a wonderful life she'd have if she stayed with him. "It sounds fabulous—and, as usual, you've thought of everything. Can I think about it? At least let me make sure I can find someone to cover me."

"What do you think of taking Friday off? Do you save your vacation for anything special? It's up to you. I just thought it would be nice to have some time to see the sights when we get to New York."

She laughed. "Oh, like this isn't special? But no, I don't. I sometimes end up using vacation days if Piper is sick more than usual, though. If we go, I'll ask for Friday off."

"Amazing! And, about the other, please don't worry your beautiful head about it."

How was she supposed to do that? Sighing, she said, "Thanks for the invite, Ethan. I'll see you tomorrow."

Apparently, she was the only crybaby of the three. The two guys were keeping it cool. Did that make what she was doing right, though? Despite being excited about Ethan's plans, she still had a niggling feeling of guilt.

Chapter Nine

Early Wednesday evening, Dallas stared anxiously out the kitchen window, waiting for the town car to pull up at her house. Opening her small bag, she checked for her lipstick—again. Meeting someone's mother hadn't been a big thing in high school. Then, it didn't matter. But Ethan was close to his mother, and tonight meant a lot to him.

Knowing his mother came from Dallas society, Dallas wore a conservative black sheath and medium heels. In her book, it was better to be too conventionally dressed than the other way around. She sighed in relief as her ride pulled up to the curb.

She locked the house as the driver got out of the car and opened her door. She smiled. Would she ever get used to this luxury?

On the drive, she racked her brain for topics of conversation that might interest his mother. Her name was Linda. Their lives were so different. Maybe Dallas's best strategy would be to have Linda talk about herself. She only hoped Ethan's mother's conversation skills equaled her son's.

Dallas took a deep breath and pushed it out. She had this. Ethan was kind—surely his mother would be too?

The car pulled up a long drive to a gorgeous house—two stories with huge walls of glass on a massive lot.

Ethan met the car as they arrived. "Dallas, come in. Mother can't wait to meet you."

He tucked her hand under his arm and led her into the...living room? Great room? Whatever it was, it was enormous.

His mother stood and intercepted them, holding out her hand. "Dallas? I'm Linda, Ethan's mother, of course. I'm so glad you could come tonight." Her obviously Botoxed smile didn't quite meet her wide, blue, plastic-surgery-enhanced eyes.

A tiny alarm bell went off in Dallas's brain. Eyeing Linda's clothes, she didn't see that the black sheath she was wearing was off the mark, so why did she sense disapproval in the other woman's expression?

Ethan led Dallas to the bar. "What would you like to drink? Mother has made some hors d'oeuvres, too."

Dallas swallowed and took a deep breath. "A Cuba Libre, please."

"A woman of simple tastes," Linda said.

Dallas turned around. "I don't usually drink anything but wine, so simple suits me. What do you like?"

Linda offered her that same confusing smile. "I often drink Manhattans. I'm having one now." Raising her glass to her son, she said, "Another, please, darling?"

Dallas took a step closer to Ethan before she realized she'd done so. It was as if her Neanderthal instincts were telling her that something threatening was on the other side of the room.

Linda had reseated herself in the middle of the sofa. This left Ethan and Dallas sitting separately in the chairs opposite.

Ethan raised his glass. "To new friends."

With a dry smile, his mother raised hers.

Dallas held up her glass. "To friends," she said, feeling as though she was standing outside a wolf den.

After taking a sip of her Manhattan, Linda asked, "So tell me, what do you do at my son's law firm?"

Ethan said, "Mother, I've already—"

"Let her talk, son. We're getting to know each other."

The predatory look in those blue eyes was all the warning Dallas needed. For some reason, this momma was spoiling for a fight. She didn't like Dallas, and she was going to pull out everything in her arsenal to turn her boy against her. "I'm an administrative assistant. I work for two of the attorneys in the office. Ethan isn't one of them."

Linda frowned. "Oh, I'm sorry. You can't make much money in that position. Ethan tells me that you have a...child? Out of wedlock? It must be hard to support a child with your salary." Laying her hand on her cheek, as if just remembering something, she said, "Wait, he also mentioned that you work at a bar? That must help out some. I'm sure the men give you big tips."

Dallas stood. "Linda, I'm not quite sure why you've decided you dislike me. I had so been looking forward to meeting you, and I adore your son. Just to be clear, I do a wonderful job rearing my daughter on the income I receive from the firm. The money I make from the club goes into an education account. I plan on completing my law degree." She turned to Ethan, who was also standing. "Would you please show me to the bathroom?"

He walked her through the house, apologizing profusely for his mother's behavior. "I've never seen her act like this. I don't know what's happened to her."

"Have you ever dated outside her"—she raised her hands in air quotes—"social group?"

He frowned.

"I thought not. That's what's going on. She thinks I'm a gold digger."

"What the hell? You're *my* choice. Mother has no say in it. She's never behaved so rudely in her life."

Dallas smiled ruefully. "She's probably never felt so threatened in her life. A child born out of wedlock? In her family? Her son, dating some poor, dumb hick?"

Ethan opened his mouth in shock. "My God, Dallas. You are not!"

"I know that. But she doesn't. I'd like to go home."

"No, Dallas. Please stay. It's important to me. Mother will behave, I promise. Take a few minutes and then join us. Everything will be fine."

Once in the lavish bathroom, Dallas sat on the cushioned bench in front of the vanity. What in holy hell had she gotten herself into? Was the woman crazy? What kind of person talked to people like that? Dallas couldn't imagine her mother ever speaking to another person that way. But then, her mother only cared that her daughter marry a man that she loved. Linda obviously had different criteria for who she wanted her son to marry.

Dallas didn't need to use the restroom. She'd just wanted to get as far away from Linda as possible. Leaning into the mirror, she applied more lipstick. Going back out there would be hell. She stared at her reflection and narrowed her eyes. *Head up, shoulders back. Ready to go.*

As Dallas entered the room, Linda rose and rushed toward her. "Dallas, please forgive me, my dear. Let's have a lovely dinner, shall we?"

Oh, how this woman loved her son. Her plastic smile was a mile from her eyes, but she *would* please Ethan. And so would

Dallas. "I'm *so* looking forward to it. Ethan said you're a fabulous cook."

Linda described what was on the menu as Ethan freshened Dallas's drink. When he came back, he said, "Mother, do you mind moving to my chair? I'd like to share the sofa with Dallas."

With just a hint of the predator, Linda smiled. "Of course, dear."

Ethan held out his hand to Dallas and pulled her in close to him as they sat down. Settling his arm around her shoulders, he asked, "So what are Piper and the nanny doing tonight?"

At the mention of her daughter, Dallas smiled. "They're picking up dinner at MacDonald's and going to the park. Piper likes playing there more than at the MacDonald's playscape now."

Ethan glanced at Linda. "I think I told you, Mother, Piper is three years old."

She took a long drink of her Manhattan and smiled stiffly. "They're so adorable at that age."

Ethan asked his mother to tell them about her most recent charity work. By the time she'd finished, mercifully, it was time for dinner.

Though the food was wonderful, Dallas's stomach was balled into a knot. She managed a few bites of everything as Linda's avid gaze examined every forkful she took. Ethan valiantly kept the conversation going, but Dallas couldn't remember spending a more miserable evening.

As they finished dinner, Linda raised her wineglass. "Shall we go to the living room for drinks?"

Ethan glanced at Dallas, and said, "Actually, Mother, I promised Dallas that I wouldn't keep her out. We never stay too late on work nights. I'll just call the car."

Linda rolled her eyes. "Of course you don't. And you always see each other on weeknights because she works at *the bar* on the weekends."

"Mother!"

Carrying her nearly empty second glass of wine, Linda left the room.

Uncharitably, Dallas figured it was most likely to make her fourth Manhattan.

Ethan shook his head. "My God, I don't know what to say. I may have her tested for dementia. Seriously."

Suddenly Dallas wanted to laugh. The woman was ridiculous. And even though it hurt, Ethan wasn't falling for her nonsense.

He clasped her hand. "Grab your wine. We'll go out on the patio."

Ethan called the driver as Dallas gazed around her in the gathering darkness. A lovely, lighted infinity pool with two rock waterfalls was the mainstay of the terrace landscaping. Flowers and flowering bushes were everywhere. She felt a little better being outside, away from Linda.

Ethan sat down beside her. "Beautiful, isn't it? I love it out here. I usually come out with a drink when I get home from work. Thank God for the pool man and the landscapers, though. It's a lot to take care of."

He reached for her hand and rubbed his thumb across hers, as was his habit, and the cold, tense feeling in her chest began to melt. This was her Ethan. He'd stood up for her. With him, she was protected, cared for, safe.

He let go of her hand, and stood. "I'm going to bring out the wine. We have about fifteen minutes. If you don't mind, I'll ride along to your house. I want some more one-on-one time with you."

"I'd like that." His arms around her were exactly what she needed right now.

When the car arrived, Dallas bid an awkward goodbye to Linda, who did the same, flashing Dallas a brief, cold smile.

As they pulled away from the house, Ethan folded her against his chest and kissed her on the forehead. "My poor Dallas. What a horrible evening. I'm so thankful that you stayed. Mother had to be shown that she couldn't run you off. I was so proud of you when you stood up to her bullying. She was an absolute disgrace. I don't know if I'll forgive her."

He tilted Dallas's chin up and kissed her. "You didn't deserve tonight. If Mother doesn't think you're worthy of me, she's wrong. You're strong, intelligent, caring, a great mother. What else should I look for in a woman? And I didn't mention that you're gorgeous. You're perfect for me."

Dallas smiled and snuggled in closer to him. "Not perfect, but thanks for the compliments. I have to be honest, Ethan. I can't in my wildest dreams imagine having Linda as permanent fixture in my life. Unless they were nightmares. No offense. I never want to go through another evening like tonight."

He turned her face so she could see him clearly. "I promise, Mother will come around. I'm everything to her. Once she knows that you're what makes me happy, she'll cave in like a sinkhole. I think you're right. She's just scared for me. I've honestly never seen her like this. She's being a protective mother bear."

Dallas couldn't bring herself to agree, but she let it go.

With the lights of the city surrounding them, Ethan looked into her eyes. "Let me make it up to you." Sliding his hand into her hair, he tilted her face to him. He kissed her eyes, her cheeks, the tip of her nose, then her lips, slowly, deeply, caressing her with his tongue.

She kissed him back. Oh, did she kiss him. She could drown in her need for him. She yanked him to her, wanting his weight on her.

He whispered in her ear, "I wish we weren't in this damn car."

Huh? She opened her eyes and took a deep breath. *Dammit. Again?* What had happened to her normal self-restraint? She kissed him softly and pulled away, sitting squarely in the seat. Maybe his mom was right. She might be a slut. For the love of... Where did her mind go when she was being kissed? Egypt? Thank God she hadn't been like this in high school. She'd never have made it to college.

Smiling, his arm around her shoulder, Ethan pulled her in close and kissed her temple.

Her pulse was still thrumming from his kisses. Damn, he was good at kissing. But his kindness was what really spoke to her. Just like he knew that she'd needed to leave tonight. Immediately. He'd rescued her with such finesse that she hadn't had to say a word. That was so like him—her protector. She leaned her head on his shoulder, thankful to have this man in her life.

* * *

Saturday morning, Cash shoved his clothes into the locker in the men's dressing room at the Cove Water Park. It was the first time he'd seen Dallas since the ruckus at the Last Cowboy, and he was hoping things went smoothly today.

He walked out into the bright sunshine and meandered over near the women's dressing-room entrance. Dallas and Piper must still be inside. Leaning against the building, he glanced around the park, which was still relatively free of people. They'd be able to get on the fun rides quickly. Movement out of the corner of his eye caught his attention, and his heart plowed into his chest wall. Dallas wore a bright turquoise bikini that showed off her rocking-hot body. He pushed away from the building and waved.

She grinned and waved back, holding Piper's hand as she walked toward him. "There you are. Where shall we go first?"

He kept his gaze safely locked on hers and away from temptation. "Let's let Piper decide." After he'd described several things around the park, the little girl chose the kids' waterslide. Clasping her little hand, he said, "This way. Come on." Dallas walked on his other side, and his breathing quickened. How in the hell would he keep his eyes off her today? Of course, he'd been attracted to her before, but this was way over the top. Did she have any idea what she did to a man in that bikini?

Dallas looked up at him and smiled. "Thanks so much for bringing us. Piper has been so excited all week. I guess you could tell that on the ride over. I should bring her, but the tickets for both of us really add up." She clasped his arm and leaned into him.

Fingers of arousal tripped up his belly, and he slung his arm around her. This was going to be an awesome day.

When they got to the waterslide, Piper eyed it, frowning, and reached for her mom's leg, curling her arm around it.

Cash squatted in front of her. "That's kind of high, isn't it? What if I went down with you? Would you like that?"

She smiled shyly and let go of her mom.

He held out his hand and stood. "Come on. Let's get in line."

Dallas smiled and mouthed *Thanks*.

When it came to their turn, Cash sat down and put Piper between his legs, wrapping his hands around her tummy. He bent and kissed her cheek as he pushed off. She screamed, then shrieked with joy the rest of the way down.

Dallas waded up to them. "Honey, that was awesome. See, it wasn't scary."

Cash helped Piper stand, handing her off to Dallas. The little girl sure looked cute in her bright-orange ruffled one-piece. "She's a brave one, all right. I'm proud of you, Piper."

As he stood, he gave a tug on Piper's sun hat. "You can do anything you put your mind to. Remember that."

Dallas flashed him a smile and a thumbs-up. "Where to next, Piper?"

Piper looked at Cash.

He took her hand and started walking. "What about the kiddie pool? That's got a lot of fun stuff."

She nodded her head and grinned.

He reached his arm around her mom again. He couldn't remember being this happy. When he glanced at Dallas, she was looking at him. Leaning down, he kissed her, enjoying the way her soft lips felt warm from the sun.

Kissing him back enthusiastically, she grinned as he lifted his head. "Thanks for being so good to Piper."

"I'll be even nicer if it gets me more of those."

She giggled. "Piper, maybe you can practice floating on your back when we get to the pool."

"Okay, Momma. Mr. Cash can help me."

He was her favorite helper now, for everything. The kid was so darn adorable. "I sure can. I remember when I learned how to float on my back." A couple with a young boy in tow walked ahead of them, and Cash realized that's what he looked like today. Glancing at Dallas and Piper, he felt a new and curious sensation settle over him. This must be what it felt like to have a family. He smiled and squeezed Dallas close. He could get used to this.

* * *

Dallas leaned back against the edge of the kiddie pool, smiling as Cash helped Piper up the slide. She'd been too timid to climb on her own. He helped her sit down, then nudged her gently down. She squealed loudly, then laughed as she slid down the slippery surface and plopped into the water at the bottom.

The guy was amazing with her daughter. The look of adoration on his face as he watched Piper slide melted Dallas's heart. This handsome man, with his beautiful ranch, had a wonderful disposition, and it showed.

Cash looked at her and grinned, and she waved to him.

He picked up Piper and walked over to Dallas. "I think we're ready for some swimming lessons."

The man had taut, tanned skin and perfectly defined slabs of muscle. Rivulets of water ran down the hard ridges of his abdomen, sending tiny shivers up her tummy.

Grinning at Piper, she asked, "Are you having fun, baby?"

She smiled and nodded.

Cash helped her daughter work on her back float for a few minutes, then settled next to Dallas. "She's a natural."

Piper wandered off and started up a conversation with another girl about her age.

Sliding his arm around Dallas's shoulder, Cash pulled her in for a quick kiss. "You and Piper make me happy."

The honest, caring look in his eyes struck something deep inside Dallas. Her heart responded with a rush of desire, and something more—an intense longing for what he seemed to be offering. She shivered.

He drew his brows together. "Cold?"

Shaking her head, she said, "I'm having a great time today too." She caressed his cheek, looked into his eyes and kissed him back, wanting him to feel how much she cared for him.

Drawing away and leaning back against the edge of the pool, she chewed her lip. When she was with Cash, it felt like he was the only man for her. Why was it, then, that when she was with Ethan, he made her feel these same things? How could she ever choose just one of them?

Chapter Ten

Cash stopped his hay pickup far inside his pasture up near Rule. Lowering the round bale on the truck's long spike to a few inches above the ground, he got out and sliced the nylon mesh surrounding it with swift strokes of his knife.

Last night, Dallas had been all he'd thought about as he lay in bed. He'd realized something that had rocked his world. He didn't just care for the woman—he was in love with her. And he didn't know what to do about it. Dallas was seeing another man, for God's sake. By her own admission, she cared for this lawyer. Then there was Piper. The little girl was starved for a man's attention. He loved her too. How in the hell had he gotten himself into a position like this? His heart had been broken once, and now he'd set himself up for that same scenario.

Wadding the mesh into a ball, he threw it into the cab and punched the button on the hydraulics, lowering the bale to the ground. It lay on its side, ready for the hungry cattle that would find it any time now. Ranch tasks like this were easy—second nature for him. Taking care of his heart was much harder. Yet, even knowing all this, he wouldn't do anything differently. He wouldn't give the woman up. His future was with Dallas and that little girl.

* * *

After picking up Piper on Friday afternoon, Dallas made a quick trip to the grocery store. She was watching her pennies today after paying the repairman to fix her fridge and washer. Having both appliances go out at once had taken a huge chunk from her monthly budget. She walked briskly behind the cart. She barely had enough time to pick up food for the weekend before getting her daughter fed, bathed, and ready to go back to her parents' house.

Most of her items were already in her basket when she turned down the dairy aisle for milk and spotted a familiar figure. She stopped her cart so fast Piper's head whipped back. *Doug.*

The man had his arm slung over a woman's shoulder in that way a cowboy had when he was in love—elbow at his girl's neck, his hand dangling down, with her head tucked in at his chin. He and the woman were peering at a grocery list while a small child sat in the seat of their cart, a lollipop in her mouth. Looking closer, Dallas noticed a sparkling wedding set on the woman's hand. Doug was married!

Whipping her basket around, Dallas sped down the next aisle, out of sight. Hot blood filled her face, her ears burned, and she wanted to punch something. She'd really liked the guy. If she hadn't already been seeing someone—*two* some-ones—she might have taken him up on his many offers to go out. Might even have fallen for him. God, she was so stupid! Gritting her teeth, she pushed her cart forward again. The lying, cheating, son of a... She needed to do something. If he were her husband, she'd want to know he was playing around.

Dallas spotted the jerk and his family two aisles over at the canned goods. Plastering a smile on her face, she walked up to the woman with an outstretched hand. "Hi, you must be Doug's sister. He comes in Friday nights at The Last Cowboy. It's wonderful to see that Doug hangs out with his niece when he can."

Ignoring Doug completely, she kept her eyes locked on the woman, who said, "I'm not his sister. I'm his wife." She turned with a confused look to Doug, whose face had lost its color.

Dallas stared at Doug. "You're married? How dare you ask me out?"

Turning to his wife, she said, "I'm so sorry, ma'am. Looks like your husband's got some explaining to do about how he spends his Friday nights."

Piper tugged on her arm. "Can we go see the toys now, Momma?"

"Sure, honey." Without looking at Doug, Dallas moved off, heading to get a gallon of milk first.

Ice-cold now, with her gut in turmoil, her thoughts went to her own situation. How could she trust Cash or Ethan? Doug was just one of many unfaithful men she'd seen at The Last Cowboy. The bar was full of disloyal jerks every weekend. How in the hell had she forgotten that?

* * *

Dallas got up early Saturday morning after a fitful night's sleep. She fixed a cup of coffee and lay on the couch, hoping to come up with the right words to cancel the day Cash had planned for the three of them. She admitted that she was frightened—scared as hell to go further in her relationship with either Cash or Ethan.

Doug had fooled her. He'd been a charming, persistent shit—exactly as if he didn't have a beautiful wife and child at home waiting for him. The creep had been a wake-up call—a dash of ice water reminding her of a man's true nature.

After fixing a second cup of coffee, she returned to the living room. Trailing her fingers along the buffet as she walked, she stopped at the photo of herself as a little girl of seven or eight. She stood in front of her mom, leaning against her and clasping her hands, desperately seeking comfort and shelter. Growing up, Dallas had always been fearful; afraid her mother would die. Terrified her father would fall asleep and never wake up.

Her mother had skipped meals when food was scarce, which was most of the time, and those awful commercials on TV talked about people starving to death. Now, as an adult, she knew that when she'd tried unsuccessfully to wake her father he'd been passed out drunk, but back then it had petrified her when he wouldn't come around. Laying the picture on her chest, she held it for a moment, wishing there had been someone to comfort that timid, frightened child with too much knowledge of life's perils.

Brushing dust off the frame, she gently placed it back where it belonged and continued on to the couch.

What if Cash and Ethan were fooling her, too? What did she really know about them? She hadn't met any of Cash's friends and didn't run in his circles. All she had was his word for his history and his character. And what about Ethan? He'd definitely been a player. His mom was always fixing him up with the daughters of her social-climber friends, too. What happened to all those women? It was too big a chance to take. And how had she let herself bring a man into her daughter's life? She'd lost her mind.

Without thinking it through, she typed the first thing that came into her head, breaking the day's date with Cash.

As soon as she tapped send, her stomach bottomed out. She'd lost something significant. Closing her eyes, she buried her face in the throw pillow. Her belly started a slow, deep burn as reality hit her. She wouldn't see Cash anymore. The light that had filled her heart ebbed away, drip by brilliant drip.

It was her choice to cut him out of her life, but that didn't matter. A dull ache settled in her chest. Her head knew that there couldn't be a relationship without trust, yet her heart wanted the man who'd been caring and kind to her. That scared little girl inside her feared being alone again.

If only she could go back to that woman who had trusted Piper's father so completely. Who had believed in his love with all her being. Until the day he'd shattered it with his uncaring words. With his decision to leave her behind like yesterday's garbage. When he'd told her that he wanted nothing to do with his child.

She opened her eyes and stared at Piper's souvenir from the train museum, which sat on the coffee table where her daughter had left it. Cash had given up his Saturday so that Dallas could spend time with Piper. Reaching out, Dallas traced the steam engine replica with her fingertip, picturing Cash holding Piper high so that she could reach the levers. Dallas folded the little engine into her palm and hugged it to her breast. Her coffee sat, untouched, until it turned cold.

* * *

Sunday came, and Dallas forced herself to be more upbeat for Piper's sake, working on the house and laundry and spending some time playing with her. Naptime finally rolled around, and

Dallas helped her daughter into bed. Though it was way too early, she poured herself a glass of wine and retreated to the couch. The simple, clean lines of her pale furniture suddenly seemed cold and unwelcoming.

Her phone rang. It was Cash. She let it go to voicemail.

Hands shaking, she picked up her phone and scrolled through her contacts. She couldn't put off telling Sarah what was going on any longer.

Her friend answered right away. "Hey, how's it going? How's Piper? No, wait, how are those two hunks you're seeing?"

Dallas couldn't help but smile a little. Her friend's bubbly personality was just what she needed. Calmer now, she answered, "Piper's great. She's taking a nap. As far as the two hunks... Sarah, I'm making a big mistake. I don't think I should see them anymore. I mean, what do I really know about them? How do I know I can trust them?" Pausing a moment, she chewed her cuticle, drawing blood.

"What happened?" Sarah sounded confused.

Dallas continued as if her friend hadn't spoken. "The fact is, I *don't* know. I've come to realize that I can't take that chance anymore."

Sarah sucked in a loud breath. "Whoa! Tell me now. What in the hell happened, honey?"

"Cash and Ethan didn't actually *do* anything." She went on to tell her friend about Doug. "It's just that it might easily have been Cash or Ethan hiding something horrible like that. How would I know?"

Sarah paused, then said, "You don't. You trust. It all comes down to that when you're in a relationship. You either trust, or you don't."

Dallas made a rude noise. "Trust? After what Piper's father did to me? I thought we'd spend the rest of our lives together. Now I feel that way about Cash and Ethan. Like maybe I might have a future with one of them. But what secrets do they hold? Will they turn their backs on me? I don't think I can take it, Sarah."

"Oh, sweetheart, you're a mess, aren't you?"

Dallas gulped long swallows of wine. "I am. I blew Cash off yesterday when he'd planned to take us out. And I'll do the same to Ethan tomorrow. I just can't face this anymore. You'd think I'd feel better now that I've decided what to do. But, Sarah?"

"Yeah, honey?"

"I thought I could just go back to the way I was, but I can't. The way I was feels terrible now. How did I ever stand my life before?" Her bottom lip trembled.

"Your life is hard. I'm not sure how you do it. Holding down two jobs and being a good momma. I have to ask—are you sure you want to do this? Break it off with Cash and Ethan?"

Dallas took another swallow of wine and rubbed the heel of her palm across her chest. "I can't find it in me to trust. I want to—but how, Sarah?"

"Trust is kind of like faith. Why don't you pray about it? I hate for you to give up on these guys. Being with them has been good for you."

Dallas closed her eyes. "Thanks for listening, Sarah. I love you."

* * *

As Dallas headed to work Monday morning, she dreaded the start of her day. What should she say to Ethan? Sarah's encouragement yesterday had done nothing but add to her confusion.

At the office, mistakes plagued her morning. Her lack of concentration and exhaustion were symptoms of her less than three hours of sleep the night before.

Finally, as she knew he would, Ethan dropped by her desk. Leaning his hip casually on the corner, he asked, "How are you, Dallas?"

Sighing, she said, "Tired. I haven't been sleeping well."

He frowned. "You okay? Can I help with anything?"

Here it was, and she had no clue what to tell him yet. "I need to slow things down a bit. Spend more time with Piper."

Ethan examined her face, searching for more than she was saying. "I'm sorry. I don't want to put any pressure on you, but I don't want to stop seeing you, either. I hope we can work this out."

This was as hard as she thought it would be. "I need some time, Ethan."

"Is this about your cowboy?" he asked, his voice strained.

She jerked her head back. "No, absolutely not. I'll always be honest with you."

He smiled and reached across the desk to clasp her hand. "Okay, then, you rest this week. Take some time, and we'll talk soon."

Really? *He* was giving *her* a week? She'd decide when she wanted to speak to him again. "I'll see you later, Ethan." Turning her back to him, she unlocked her computer and got back to work.

At three o'clock, Cash sent her a text. *I'm missing you today. I hate it when I don't see you on the weekend. Hope you're having a great Monday.*

She sent a happy face back. If only she knew how to trust Cash—trust Ethan. She couldn't just snap her fingers and make it happen. Following Sarah's advice, she'd prayed last night. So far, nothing had changed.

That afternoon, as she headed to the copy room, Dallas heard Ethan's voice coming from his assistant's desk. The unpleasant tone made her pause and listen.

"How am I supposed to show this to my client? The colors are all wrong. I told you how I wanted it. My meeting's in ten minutes, and there's no time to change it. This is an embarrassment!"

Ethan stormed out of his office and into Dallas's line of sight. His angry expression softened into a welcoming one as he approached her. "Hey, what's up?"

Uneasy after what she'd overheard, she said, "I'm on my way to make some copies. See you." She moved around him, hurrying down the hall. Never had she heard him use that tone of voice. Was he having a really bad day, or did Ethan behave like that regularly? Deeply unsettled, she finished her copies and made her way back to her desk. A terrible thought hit her as she sat down. If, in the end, she chose Cash, would Ethan treat her badly too?

By the time she'd picked up Piper and driven home, she was having a hard time putting one foot in front of the other. She microwaved macaroni and cheese for her daughter, gave her several dollops of applesauce and a glass of milk, and called it dinner. Piper watched cartoons and played with her toys while Dallas drowsed on the couch. Her pulse slowed as her mind gradually numbed.

After Piper's bath, Dallas read her a story and tucked her in. Her own bed pulled at her. Even her usual glass of wine didn't sound good. She dropped her head onto her pillow, feeling drugged although she hadn't taken anything. A few minutes later, her phone rang. The caller's name filled her with dread. *Cash.* Dropping the cell unanswered on the nightstand, she turned over, grasping for the reprieve of sleep.

* * *

Tuesday afternoon, after moving through her day like a sleepwalker, she arrived home with Piper, determined to get her fed and ready for bed early. Her phone rang as she lay on the couch while her daughter ate dinner in the kitchen. Heart sinking, Dallas read *Cash* on the caller ID. She couldn't dodge him anymore. Picking up, she said, "Hi, Cash. How are you?"

"Worried." His voice, full of anxiety, sounded loud over the line. "You haven't answered my calls. Is everything okay?"

Telling Cash that she needed to spend more time with Piper didn't seem right. He always went out of his way to include her daughter in the time they spent together. With an overwhelming need to be honest, she said, "It's...ah... I'm having a hard time..." God, how could she say she didn't trust him? It sounded so wrong.

"What is it, honey? Let me help you." His concern came through loud and clear.

She signed heavily. There was no way to make this sound nice. "Something's happened. I mean, I don't really know you at all. I don't know that I can trust—"

"I'm coming over." He hung up.

God, what had she done? The last thing she wanted was to meet him face-to-face. Every muscle in her body felt limp, lifeless. She couldn't see Cash. Not like this. Not tonight.

Piper walked in. "I'm done, Mommy. Can I watch cartoons now?"

"How about we take your bath first, honey." Escorting her daughter to the bathroom, she searched every inch of her being for the strength to face the man who'd be knocking at her door in an hour.

* * *

With his mind fractured into a million crazy thoughts, Cash sped toward Dallas's house. What the hell was the woman thinking? She didn't know him? Didn't know if she could trust him? Where in God's name had that come from? She might as well have hit him with a shovel. *Dammit.* He'd done nothing to give her cause to doubt him.

He shook his head, gritting his teeth. Her past few days of silence, except for that damn happy face, had driven him crazy. He'd imagined all sorts of awful things happening, the worst of which was that she'd dumped him and chosen the lawyer. He pressed his lips together. It could still be that, couldn't it? She might have been spouting excuses on the phone. Gusting out a breath, he rubbed his forehead hard. He really hoped not. He loved Dallas. No way was he losing her to that freaking guy.

Later, after knocking firmly on Dallas's door, he promised himself that he would be calm and listen to what she had to say, despite his frustration.

She opened the door, and the first thing that popped into his mind was that she looked bedraggled. He instantly shifted gears from angry and hurt to extremely concerned for her. Drawing his brows together, all he could think to say was, "Hey."

"Hey."

Everything he'd planned on saying now felt wrong. He had to forget about his own feelings and find out what she was going through.

As he entered, the house was quiet. "Where's Piper?"

"I put her to bed a little earlier tonight so we could talk."

He followed her to the living room and sat on the couch, giving her plenty of space. "So, tell me, what's worrying you?"

Dallas eased down on the cushion and pulled a throw pillow against her stomach, her eyes downcast. "I'm sorry you came all this way tonight, Cash."

Frustrated, he said more sharply than he meant to, "I had to, dammit." He sighed and went on calmly, "Dallas, I don't think you know how much you mean to me. Will you tell me what's wrong?"

Her fingers tightened on the pillow. "There's this guy...he..." Her voice trailed off and she looked away from him, as if frustrated.

He clenched his fists. "What? Did he hurt you?" His pulse pounded.

She looked up with a startled expression. "No, no, that's not it."

He blew out a hard breath and unclenched his hands, urging her, "Start from the very beginning."

Picking at the design on the colorful pillow, she slowly told him about seeing Doug and how angry his betrayal had made her. "Suddenly I thought, how do I know I can trust Cash or Ethan? Everything I believe about them could be lies."

She paused to gather her thoughts. "Cash, I lived with Piper's father for a year and a half, and he planned to leave me and move back east without telling me. And, after saying for two years how much he loved me, when I got pregnant, he wanted nothing to do with my baby. How am I supposed to trust? I never saw any of that coming, and it nearly destroyed me. I can't trust right now. Not you or Ethan."

Her eyes were red with tears. It was all Cash could do to keep from pulling Dallas into his arms and comforting her as she spoke, but he had a feeling that doing so wouldn't be right. She needed to stand on her own two feet while she faced up to her feelings.

He slid a little closer to her and picked up her hand. It was icy cold, and he sandwiched her fingers between his warm ones. God, how he wanted to take care of this woman. "Dallas, I've been betrayed before, and it hurts. Loss of trust is a hard thing. It kills love. But the thing here is, I've done nothing to lose your trust. You're operating on fear and a previous bad experience. I'm not saying I blame you. You've had it rough." He squeezed her hand. "I just don't want to lose you because of it."

Eyes downcast, she said, "I understand how unfair my feelings are, but how do I change them? I've tried. I've prayed about it, but these thoughts run round and round in my head." She looked into his eyes.

Now he scooted beside her and pulled her against him. Nestling her head under his chin, he said quietly, "Feel my arms around you. Listen to my heartbeat. Hear me when I say I'll never betray you." He kissed her forehead and closed his eyes, letting the silence seal his words.

* * *

The following Sunday rolled around, and Dallas was more herself. She'd done a lot of soul searching, some of it pretty painful, though her conversation with Cash had helped more than anything to dispel her distrust. His promise touched her deeply, forging a new and stronger bond between them.

True to his word, Ethan had allowed her space, and she felt better about being with him again too.

Kate and Sarah were coming over at three for wine and cheese and some much-needed girl talk. Sarah was bringing her two kids, six-year-old Colin and three-year-old Cara, and Piper was ecstatic about having someone to play with.

At noon Sarah called. "Hey, Dallas, you ready for two rowdy munchkins this afternoon?"

Dallas laughed. "Yours will fit right in with mine. She's so excited she probably won't take her nap."

"You're lucky. I can't get my two to lay down anymore at all. Hey, listen, remember when we talked about Acacia?"

"Sure."

"She's been swamped with last-minute wedding plans. I thought I'd bring her along today, if you don't mind. She's agreed to be my designated driver, too."

"Oh, I'd love to see her. Of course she's welcome."

#

Dallas finished tidying the house and had time to get herself cleaned up before Kate arrived at the door holding up a bottle. Dallas leaned in for a kiss. "Thanks for the wine. You know what I like."

Kate laughed. "How are you?" Narrowing her eyes, she took in every detail of her friend's face. "You need to get more sleep, woman. You're getting crow's feet."

Dallas grinned. "Oh, just what I wanted to hear. I've lost some sleep, but I'm better now. Hopefully they'll go away." Thinking of Ethan's mother, she laughed. "Botox is *not* an option."

Piper wiggled between them, reaching her hands in the air. "Hi, Auntie Kate."

The woman smiled and lifted the little girl into her arms, following her hostess to the kitchen.

After opening the wine, Dallas poured them each a glass. Taking a sip, she asked, "What have you been doing? It seems like ages since we talked."

Kate launched into a tale of her most recent shenanigans—who she was dating and where they'd gone.

Dallas smiled as she listened. Honestly, she couldn't imagine a future where Kate settled down with one man and got married. She enjoyed being chased too much. The beautiful young woman had her pick of men and loved going out and traveling to new places. Neither could Dallas see Kate as a mother. Rolling her eyes, Dallas envisioned Kate with barf on her dress as she bottle-fed a baby. No way. Wouldn't happen.

A knock sounded, and Dallas went to the door.

Sarah, full of energy, as always, swept in and headed to the kitchen, trailing Acacia in her wake. The kids headed to the backyard.

Dallas drew Acacia into a hug. Her dark brown hair and eyes set off her pale skin in a striking way. Dallas had forgotten how gorgeous she was. Pulling back, Dallas asked, "How are you? I hear you're getting married."

She grinned. "I didn't realize how much work organizing a wedding was when I started all this. If I had known, I would have eloped."

Dallas laughed and pulled her into the kitchen, pouring her a glass of iced lemon water. "Let's all go outside where the kids can play and stay out of our hair."

With a chorus of "Yes!" the women joined the kids in the backyard.

Holding the cheese-and-crackers tray, Dallas led the women to the chairs and tables under the shade trees. "I'm so glad you all could come. We need to do this more often."

Sarah lifted her glass. "Hear, hear."

"So, Acacia, tell us all about your honeymoon and where you're going to live. You know, everything!" Kate said.

"Johnny's keeping mum about the honeymoon. But afterwards, we'll live on his family ranch. We've been looking at house plans with a builder, and I'm excited. I want my kids to grow up on a ranch like I did." She smiled, and a flush crept up the pale skin of her neck. "Not that we plan on children right away."

Sarah laughed. "Take it from me, girl. Have *lots* of fun first."

Acacia giggled.

Cara jogged up to her momma. "Colin won't share the ball. It's my turn."

Shaking her head, Sarah called, "Colin, let your sister have a turn, or you'll have to come listen to girl talk for ten whole minutes!"

Cara ran back to join the play.

Sarah motioned to Dallas with her wineglass. "Speak, girl. How is everything with your two hunks. Better now?"

"Yeah." An immediate bubble of happiness tickled her chest. Thank goodness Cash had talked some sense into her. She would have lost...well, lost everything that had made her life so joyful recently.

Sarah launched into a remix of her past week and had everyone giggling.

As the evening went on, Dallas leaned back in her chair and looked at her friends one by one. She'd been too shy and insecure to make friends when she was young. She'd missed out on so much. This was what made life worthwhile—sharing time with people you loved.

She would soon have to make a choice between two very special men. She could only share her future with one of them.

Chapter Eleven

Ethan filled his plate at the Chinese buffet near the office. Dallas was in line just ahead of him. He'd asked her to lunch with an agenda in mind. He was hoping she'd agree to another overnight date with him. Separate rooms, of course. He wouldn't pressure her at this stage in the game. Sharing a room would come, though. He'd make sure of that.

A moment later, he joined Dallas at their table. "How's Piper these days?" he asked.

"She's great. Growing out of all her clothes. I think she's going to be tall like her father." A frown flitted across her face, and she took a quick bite of her food.

Ethan reached across the table and clasped her hand. "I came across some symphony tickets, and I hope you'll come with me. It's the weekend after next. We'd drive up to Dallas Saturday morning and return Sunday evening. Please say you'll come. We'll have such fun." He examined her expression closely, hoping for enthusiasm—or at least a sign that she was open to the idea.

Dallas looked over his shoulder, her eyes faraway. The corner of her mouth lifted. "I've always wanted to go to the symphony." Taking another bite, she chewed a moment, then said, "Let me see what my parents have to say. And I need to find someone to cover for me Saturday night at The Last Cowboy." She smiled into his eyes. "I'd love to go if I can work things out."

Ethan grinned. "Wonderful! I'll plan everything. I hope Piper and the nanny can find some fun things to do as well."

Thank God the girl didn't mind staying with the nannies at the service. That had been a stroke of genius on his part. It was too bad Dallas had gotten pregnant so young. It was hard on her, as a single mom, to have to make plans for a child every time she wanted to do something on her own.

He was glad he hadn't had children yet. He knew he would have to at some point as the sole heir in his family, but by then he planned on being married, and his wife would handle all the care. He'd be busy furthering his career. His current partnership was merely a step toward a better one at a larger law firm somewhere in Dallas, closer to his mother. He already had a nibble at a very prestigious opportunity. This plan didn't need to be revealed to the woman sitting across from him, though. Not yet, anyway. Not until she fell for him. It did, however, mean that time was of the essence. His plans for beautiful Dallas had to move forward as quickly as possible.

That meant meeting her daughter. He needed to gain the child's goodwill before he could seal the deal with Dallas. The girl was sure to be a good little thing. After all, look at her mother. It shouldn't be too hard to establish a connection with...Pippi? Piper? Pepper? It was one of those silly names. "Can I ask a favor?"

She met his gaze. "Sure."

"Would you introduce me to your daughter soon?"

Her eyes filled with warmth. "I'd like that."

"Perhaps we can all go for ice cream."

"Piper would love it. How about Saturday after her nap? Say two o'clock?"

Piper. That was the child's name. He'd write it down when he got to his office. "It's a date, then. I'm looking forward to it."

As they walked the few blocks back to work, Ethan smiled. Surely he was leaps and bounds ahead of the other guy in Dallas's affections. She was a smart woman. She'd realize that he had much more to offer than any cowboy. Ethan slipped his arm around her waist, kissing her behind the ear and claiming what he already felt was his.

* * *

Saturday afternoon, Dallas glanced over as Piper licked her banana cone in the Braum's ice-cream shop near their house. Ethan's wide-eyed gaze was locked on Piper's face, which was smeared with goo. Dallas grabbed a napkin and wiped the stuff off before it could drip. Hadn't the guy seen a child eat ice cream before? Now the cone was dripping on Piper's hand. *Hell!* Grabbing more napkins, she wrapped the cone in several layers and handed it back to her daughter.

Ethan cleared his throat and said in a bright voice, "Piper, what do you like to do for fun?"

The little girl stared at him. She'd been quiet since Ethan had told her sternly on the ride over to please stop kicking his seat. She finally said, "Doggies."

He drew his brows together and glanced at Dallas. "Doggies?"

Shrugging, she said, "Maybe she means my parents' dog?"

Ethan tried again. "You like to play with your grandparents' dog?"

Piper licked her lips and slowly shook her head no.

Dallas sighed. "Piper, use your words. What doggies?"

She turned to her mom, her eyes wide and innocent.

Ethan smiled uncomfortably and shrugged. "It's fine. Kids will be kids."

While they finished their ice cream, Ethan talked about a vacation to Rio he'd taken one year. Piper was silent.

As Dallas gathered the used napkins and trash, Piper said, "I want to go to the park."

Ethan, who'd begun to rise, froze.

Dallas glanced over and said, "That's up to Ethan."

He tilted the corner of his mouth up. "Uh, no problem."

Not the most enthusiastic response Dallas could imagine, but he was willing, she'd give him that. It was obvious that he didn't have much experience with kids. But Cash had said that he didn't either, and look how great he was with Piper.

Ethan took the tray full of trash and dumped it, and they headed for his car.

That was another thing. His two-door sports car was a pain when it came to putting Piper's car seat in the back. Ethan had had to pull the belts from beneath the seat because they'd never been used. If Dallas wasn't mistaken, he'd swallowed a few choice words before everything was firmly in place. Strapping Piper in was no picnic, either.

Once they got to the park, her daughter seemed more relaxed. She ran to the swings and called, "Push me, Mr. Keys."

Ethan glanced at Dallas with startled eyes.

She laughed. "Go ahead, Mr. Keys. It's my turn to rest. I do this all the time."

He helped the little girl up into the swing and, with a small push, set her moving.

"No. Harder," Piper said, in a disgusted voice.

The next time he pushed her a little higher, and Piper was quiet.

Dallas sighed. The poor man. He couldn't be more out of his element if he were at the bottom of the sea.

Soon, Piper called, "I want to slide."

Ethan pulled her to a stop, and she slid out of the swing and headed to the playscape.

Ethan turned around, reminding Dallas of a dog with his soulful, begging eyes. But she wanted to see what the man was made of. With a shooing motion, she said, "Go, go. She needs help. I'll watch you from here."

Sighing, he gave her a quick smile. Stuffing his hands in his pockets he walked after Piper.

The little girl climbed the wooden fort and twirled the steering wheel, ignoring Ethan.

He stood quietly, watching.

Suddenly she was at the top of the slide and pushing off, yelling, "Catch me!"

Snatching his hands out of his pockets, he lurched for the bottom of the slide. He was too late.

"Ouch!" Piper yelled, as she landed on her backside. She pouted, thrusting out her lip as she glared at Ethan.

He picked her up and dusted off her shorts. "I'm so sorry. Let me take you to your mother."

Dallas observed it all with narrowed eyes. Her little turkey was playing games. She knew how to land on her feet when she went down the slide. Dallas yelled, "Ethan, she's just fine. That wasn't your fault."

Piper sat stiffly in Ethan's arms as he walked back toward her.

Dallas picked up her purse and sighed. This day had not gone well at all.

* * *

After Ethan dropped them at the house, Piper was Dallas's shadow, following her from room to room until it was time to go to her grandparents' house. Dallas had even rocked her while she read her a book.

Piper's unusual behavior kept coming back to Dallas as she tended bar that night. She wasn't sure if Piper disliked Ethan or if she was just uncomfortable with him. Maybe she felt he was trying to take Cash's place. Dallas knew having two men in her life was complicated, but it looked like it might also be disruptive for her daughter. She couldn't have that. Somehow, some way, she had to choose.

* * *

Sunday morning, Cash slid the steaks into his homemade marinade, sealing the lid before putting them in the fridge. He had a lot riding on today. Dallas and Piper were on their way to spend the day with him, and he was determined to make Dallas his before she went home. He'd thought it all through and had come to the conclusion that he'd been way too relaxed in his approach to their relationship. Tired of being patient, he'd decided that he needed to take control of the whole two-man situation and show Dallas just how much he cared.

He headed down to the barn, where two of his horses stood ready in stalls. Yesterday, to save time this morning, he'd brought them up from the pasture. As he brushed each one down, he went over his strategy. By the time they were saddled, he heard Dallas's car drive up. Mounting Rambo, he jogged toward the house.

Dallas stepped out of the car as he approached, the sun boldly highlighting her long blond hair. His Blue Heeler cowdog wiggled his butt and begged for attention. As she bent down to pet him, Cash called out, "Say hi to Blue Boy."

Pulling the horse to a stop in front of her, he said, "Dallas, meet Rambo, your ride for the day."

Taking a step back, she eyed the animal. "He's kind of big, isn't he?"

"Naw, my horse is bigger. Rambo's just right."

Piper cried, "I want out, Momma."

Dallas opened the back door and released her daughter from her car seat. "You stay close to me, honey. I don't want you to get kicked."

"Hey, Rambo's got manners. He won't kick," Cash said, in a wounded voice.

Piper held her arms up to Cash. "I want a ride, please, Mr. Cash?"

He raised his brows and looked at Dallas.

"All right, but be careful with my baby."

Cash pulled the little girl from Dallas's arms and settled her in front of him. "There're cold drinks in the fridge, and I put a fresh pot of coffee on. Make yourself comfortable while me and my sweetie here take a ride."

Dallas chewed her lip and nodded.

Nudging Rambo with his heels, they turned toward the barn.

Piper clutched the horn and yelled, "Yippee!"

Cash grinned. She felt so fragile—didn't weigh more than a bug's fart, as his grandfather used to say. He stroked one of her little pigtails with his finger. Was there anything in the world more precious than this tiny person?

They passed the barn, and he turned down the lane that led to a bunch of old rusty tanks, some as tall as twenty feet. At one time, there'd been oil pumped out of this land. But when the price had dropped, his father had stopped production and sealed the wells. The ground still bore scars from those days where nothing would grow.

Details he seldom spotted anymore caught Piper's attention. "What's that brown stuff on the road?"

He grinned. "That's cow poop."

"Yukky. It's big."

"Yep."

"How come Rambo makes that sound when he walks?"

"Because he has hard shoes on his feet."

"Oh. I don't want shoes like that."

"Me neither."

"I like your butterflies. You have lots of butterflies."

How come he'd never noticed that? She was right, though. He looked around and counted three without even trying. "They're pretty, huh?"

"Yeah."

And so their ride went. By the time they returned to the house, he was enchanted. How had he lived this long and not realized how much he wanted a child? Tying Rambo to a shady oak tree in the yard, he picked up Piper and held her in his arms. "Let's go find Momma."

Dallas sat on the sofa in the living room drinking a cup of coffee and reading his book on the history of Haskell County. She smiled and held it up. "Your family is in this."

"Yeah, we've been here a while. There're quite a few of the original pioneer families still ranching in this area. My friend Ward Ramsey's family is in there, too. We grew up together, and his ranch butts up to mine."

Shaking her head, she said, "It's like something out of a Zane Grey book."

He sat down next to her and settled Piper on his lap.

The little girl snuggled into his chest.

He put his arm around Dallas, giving her a quick kiss. "Well, one thing's for sure. I always knew how I'd make my living. I can't imagine spending my life doing anything else."

She leaned her head on his shoulder and cupped Piper's face. "Did you have fun on your ride?"

Piper giggled, playing with the buttons on Cash's shirt-sleeve. "We saw butterflies and cow poop."

Dallas laughed. "Really?"

"Uh-huh, and Mr. Cash says I can ride by myself in the ca...ca..."

"Corral." He kissed her cheek. "That's right. But when we go anywhere else, you sit with me." He wasn't taking any chances with this precious little bundle.

Dallas wrinkled her forehead at this revelation but didn't say anything.

Cash reassured her. "I'll lead her around."

Dallas let out a breath. "Good. Horses are just so big."

"I guess they are. I don't notice anymore. She'll be fine."

Piper crawled into Dallas's lap. "I'm hungry, Momma."

Cash said, "I've got sandwich fixings for lunch, and I'm barbecuing steaks later. Come on into the kitchen."

Piper yawned several times while she ate, though her curiosity kept her asking questions.

When the little girl was finished eating, Dallas scooted back her chair. "Naptime, baby girl. You'll need lots of energy for our horse ride this afternoon."

Piper's frown instantly turned into a smile at the mention of another horse ride.

"I'll show you where she can sleep."

Dallas hesitated. "I may need to rock her some. She's wound up, and it's a strange place."

"How about I bring a rocker to the room?"

She smiled. "Perfect. Thanks."

While Dallas put Piper to sleep, Cash cleaned up the kitchen. His chest tightened as he thought of having at least an hour with Dallas all to himself. Now he'd show her in every way how much he cared for her—how he wanted her. He couldn't lose the woman he loved for lack of trying.

Thirty minutes later, Dallas found him on the couch where he'd been fidgeting, hoping she would be receptive to the warm, seductive kisses he couldn't wait to give her. Admitting to a little insecurity had been hard for him, but it was true. Between work and their dates, Dallas spent a lot of time with the lawyer. Cash stood and pulled Dallas into his arms. "Is our girl asleep?"

"I thought she'd never close her eyes. She's so excited." Dallas grinned at him. "You're her hero, but I guess you know that. I finally had to threaten there'd be no horse ride before she relaxed and fell asleep. I hated to do it but, trust me, you don't want to be around that little hellion this evening if she skips a nap."

Laughing, he said, "Hellion?"

"You bet."

His fingertip traced the outline of her lip.

She leaned into him.

He took a relieved breath. Dallas wanted him too. Cupping her head, he brushed his lips to hers.

She sighed softly.

His pulse raced as he pulled her tight against him. His kisses were slow, deep, and coaxing. He needed her to want him as much as he wanted her.

She kissed him back, lifting up on her toes to reach his lips and sliding her hands around his neck.

As her fingers ran through his hair, he took control of the kiss, possessive, greedy, delving deep and caressing her tongue. Shit, she was making him hard.

She pulled him down to her with a kiss so hot his hands trembled. God, didn't she say she wanted to take things slow?

Easing back, he feathered kisses across her lips, changing the tempo, giving her time to find herself again.

She darted her tongue between his lips, and his heart lurched into full speed again. They tasted each other deeply, and he moaned. God, this woman was testing every ounce of his restraint.

He pulled her down with him to lie on the sofa, stretching her across his length, giving her the power to break off at any time.

Looking into her eyes, he brushed her hair from her cheek.

She stared back with a small, dazed smile.

He clasped her waist and slid her farther up on his chest. Her lips were now kissably close. "I want you, Dallas. At some point, this situation has to end. You know that. I hope someday soon you'll choose me." Running his thumb across her plump lower lip, he said, "It'll be the best day of my life."

Before she could answer, he pulled her to him. His kiss was tender, sweet. He needed her to feel how cherished she'd be every day.

He slid his tongue into her mouth, deepening the kiss, caressing her as his pulse ramped up. He couldn't help it. There was no stopping kissing the woman when he had her this close. Cupping her head in his hands, he claimed her lips, thrusting all else from his mind.

Her full, taut breasts pushed against him. He wanted her. Growling, he grabbed her hips and dragged her across the bulge at his zipper.

She pulled back from him just as he realized what he'd done and froze.

He whispered, "Oops." The pupils of her eyes were so dilated he could hardly see the irises. *My God, she's so damn sexy.* "I don't think that was exactly taking it slow. Sorry."

She laughed shortly and licked her lips. "What did you say? It takes two?" Leaning her head against his chest, she said, "I like kissing you."

He tipped her chin so that he could look into her eyes. "I didn't want to stop. I want you, Dallas. But when you're ready. Not before. I know I'm the one for you. I can give you what you need. The life that will make you and Piper happy. I just need you to discover that for yourself."

She snuggled closer. "I can't even imagine what this situation must be like for you. I want you to know that I really care for you too. I mean that. If it helps, when I'm with you like this, I just *know* you're the man I want to be with."

He frowned. "Then you see your lawyer and get all confused again."

She sighed, lines appearing in her forehead. "It's awful. I can't tell you how confusing it is. I end up feeling guilty half the time. I've never experienced anything like it. I promise I'll figure it out."

He patted her, keeping his expression neutral. They snuggled, near sleep, until Piper woke from her nap.

They spent the afternoon on horseback. Piper got to ride by herself in the corral, declaring that she was a cowgirl by the time she was finished. Cash had Dallas ride in the corral for a little while until she got comfortable giving the horse commands, and then they rode all over the home pasture.

Cash had a big backyard where he barbecued the steaks, roasted corn, and even baked potatoes on the pit. By the time the oranges and reds of sunset streaked the horizon, they all had full stomachs. Piper played chase with Blue Boy. The dog seemed tickled to know someone who actually liked being chased.

Cash pulled Dallas into his lap. Their lawn chairs faced the colorful evening sky. "I've had the best day. I wish you were mine. You'd never have to leave. Just think of all the bedrooms Piper has to choose from."

Dallas cracked up. "Well, that is a selling point I hadn't thought of." She cupped his cheek and brushed a soft kiss across his lips. "I had a wonderful day, too. You have a beautiful home here. I love it."

"Well, the house has character, and the ranch is beautiful." He caught her gaze and held it. "Dallas, I want my children raised here where they know their neighbors and the kids they go to school with. My kids will grow up loving animals and the land. They'll go to church with me and love God like I do. They'll learn to respect their elders and be proud of their country." He held her fingers to his lips and kissed them. "Our children would have that life, Dallas."

She wrapped her arms around his neck and whispered, "You're offering me the world, and I know it. Thank you, Cash." As she nestled her head on his shoulder, the last colors of the sunset faded.

Darkness settled over them, and Cash squeezed her. "Before you go, I want to tell you something. You never let me explain about the girl who kissed me at the club."

She stiffened in his arms but held still.

"She had no right to do that. She's one of Jesse's ex-girlfriends. That girl was always coming on to me, even while she was dating him. She was drunk. I sure didn't want her kiss or her piling into my lap. I'm so sorry you had to see it."

Dallas didn't say anything, but she gave him a quick kiss, and he knew he was forgiven.

Patting her leg, he said, "You'd better get on the road. Deer are a menace this time of night."

He helped her gather Piper's bag and toys and load her into the car. Not caring that Piper's eager eyes were watching, he pulled Dallas in for a lingering kiss. When he drew back, he looked her in the eyes. "You think on today, long and hard, Dallas. You'll know in your heart who to choose."

She bit her lip, looking torn. "Oh, Cash..."

Kissing her cheek, he said, "Go on, now. Get home safe."

* * *

That night, Dallas turned over for the umpteenth time, her mind racing. Piper had fallen asleep in the car and didn't wake when Dallas put her to bed. It being a work night, Dallas had gone to bed shortly after. But her thoughts tormented her, keeping her awake.

Everything about her day with Cash had affected her deeply. He'd acted like a different man, leaving her in no doubt as to what he wanted. She'd been overwhelmed. She was the luckiest woman alive to have Cash Powers care about her. And yet, here she was, unable to accept what he offered. At least, not now.

She had to think about Piper's future. Ethan could offer her daughter a fantastical world. A world of wealth and travel. An expensive education. Piper could become anything she could imagine. Ethan had the financial resources to provide everything for her daughter that Dallas had ever dreamed of as a child.

And he was such a good, kind man. Sexy, too. Dallas remembered the passion he'd aroused in her on the couch in their suite in California and the way she hadn't been able to keep her hands off him in the town car as they'd driven back to her house. And, after he'd rescued her from his mom, she'd felt so protected and cherished. Yes, Ethan, too, was someone she could definitely see herself spending the rest of her life with.

Every aching breath she took told her she had to choose soon.

Flipping herself over again, she jammed the pillow under her neck. What the hell was wrong with her? How could she feel so strongly about two men at the same damn time? She couldn't bear to hurt either one of them. Yet she could see that coming, and she couldn't stand it.

But in the end, she would have to choose. She would have to break the heart of a good man.

Chapter Twelve

Dallas finished the last bite of her meal and wiped her hands on a napkin. Ethan had packed a wonderful lunch for the drive to the city. The symphony started at seven-thirty, but they'd planned on arriving early to give themselves plenty of time to check in at the hotel and dress.

He passed her a glass of wine. "I can't tell you how much I look forward to having you to myself this weekend." He tapped his glass with hers. "To beautiful music and desire."

She smiled. "To my first symphony and a night to be someone other than Mommy."

"Tonight, I promise you, when I hold you in my arms you definitely won't feel like a mommy." The look in his eyes and his wicked smile left her in no doubt as to his meaning.

Her lips parted as she leaned toward him. This handsome man, so kind to her in every way, reached into the center of her being, answering an elemental yearning that had crushed her from her earliest memories. That terrible craving came from poverty—from never, ever having enough. With Ethan, she was safe from hunger, from unmet needs, from nameless want. He had everything she'd ever wished for. She touched his face. "I don't thank you enough for the kind things you do for me. I'm looking forward to this weekend."

He leaned in, brushing the softest, feathery kisses across her lips. Pulling back, he caught her gaze. "I love taking care of you. I want to spend the rest of my life finding ways to make your life better. You need to understand that, Dallas."

Like balm on a scraped knee, his words eased her. Smiling, she sat back in the seat and closed her eyes. The thrum of the car's powerful engine lulled her.

A moment later, Ethan clasped her hand.

She opened her eyes and took a sip of wine. Squeezing his fingers, she stared out the window. This would be a wonderful life. She'd never want for anything. He would cherish her, and Piper would have the best of everything. How could she not choose Ethan?

\#

Just after seven, with Dallas on his arm, Ethan walked toward their box near the stage. His family had kept it for years. Men were staring at Dallas, and no wonder. The long, emerald-green, off-the-shoulder gown fit every contour of her stunning figure. With her hair piled high on her head, leaving loose strands to curl around her face and neck, there wasn't a more beautiful woman in the room. And she was his. He was damned if he wouldn't do everything in his power this weekend to make sure she chose him. As they arrived at their seats, he slid his arm around her waist and ushered her into the box. They had it to themselves tonight.

A waitress came by a few minutes later, and he ordered wine.

Dallas's eyes were glued to the stage where the musicians were tuning their instruments and chatting quietly with one another, making a wild mishmash of sounds.

He caught her gaze, and she grinned at him. Clasping her hand, he asked, "What do you think?"

Excitement bled through her fingers, and she answered in a rush. "I didn't know there were so many people in a symphony. I can't wait until they start."

The wine arrived, and he handed her a glass. "The lights go out, and it's dark except for the stage. Your whole world becomes the music. I lose myself in it every time. I can't help it."

Her eyes widened, and she sighed. "Oh, Ethan. How lucky you are to enjoy nights like this in your life."

He slid his arm around her. "I'm lucky to have nights like this *with you* in my life."

She kissed his cheek and looked out over the stage again.

He couldn't take his eyes off her. Her beautiful face, long slender neck, and those full breasts pushing up from the scooping neckline of the dress were like a siren's call. His fingers itched to touch every inch of her gorgeous body. Not tonight, though. She wasn't quite there yet. New York, on the other hand, would be a different story. If he had his way, and he was sure he would, his time with her there would be something else entirely.

The hall quieted as the conductor came on stage. The crowd applauded with enthusiasm, and he bowed. As the man gathered the attention of the musicians, Ethan glanced at Dallas. The music began, and she leaned forward, her eyes wide and that beautiful mouth of hers slightly open. He wanted to kiss those full lips and drive everything but thoughts of him from her mind. He set his chin on his steepled hands. There would be time for that. Let her enjoy this first taste of exquisite music.

At the end of the evening, when the last note sounded, Dallas closed her eyes, clasping her hands to her breast. "Ethan, this was the most beautiful night I've ever spent. I'll never be able to thank you enough."

He brushed her cheek with his knuckles. "I loved watching you enjoy it. We have dinner reservations. Are you hungry?"

She raised her brows and laughed. "I just realized I'm famished."

"Come on, then."

He'd already texted the driver, and their limo was outside waiting for them. The restaurant was close and, in no time, they were seated at a table sipping wine.

Ethan glanced over his menu and asked, "Are you tired?"

"I am, and I can't understand why. It's like I've run a marathon or something."

Laughing, he said, "You lived every note of that music. It's no wonder."

"I'll sure sleep well tonight."

He smothered a smile. That depended. He might have her so revved up before he turned her loose that it would take hours for her to fall asleep. She'd accept his marriage proposal when it came. He'd make sure of that.

They didn't dawdle over dinner, and he pulled Dallas into his arms as they rode back to the hotel.

Closing her eyes, she snuggled into him and relaxed.

He planted tiny kisses on her forehead, and she lifted her mouth to his, her eyes still closed. His belly tightened. She looked so damned vulnerable like that, and infinitely more desirable. Her lips were petal-soft. He shivered, the intensity of his need pulsing through him. Yet he slowed. Tracing the seam of her lips with the tip of his tongue, he withdrew.

Her eyes had stayed closed. She was still waiting for his touch.

He breathed a tiny breath in her ear and landed the lightest little kiss on the sensitive spot behind it.

A shiver ran through her.

Yes. Tremble, Dallas. Want me. As he lowered his lips to hers, she opened to his soft, coaxing kisses. He worshipped her mouth with his tongue.

She cupped his face, teasing him with a kiss of her own.

It nearly drove him to lose control. They must be near the hotel. He kissed her hard, then softly, then hard again. When he pulled back, she was breathing in quick pants. She wanted more, and that was how he'd leave her until they got back to the suite. Clasping her cheek in his hand, he ran his thumb across her lower lip. "Dallas, you're an amazing woman."

She breathed deeply, and sat back against the seat. "Oh, Lord. You do know how to kiss a girl, Ethan Keys."

Once at the hotel, he opened their door, and turned to her. "Join me in a nightcap. Please?"

Smiling, she walked past him into the room. "One glass, then. I'm tired. I wish it weren't too late to call and check on Piper."

He inserted the wine opener into the bottle that he'd left on the table before they set out for the symphony. "Come on. Remember, you're not a mommy tonight."

She grinned. "Oh, right."

After pouring them each a glass, he joined Dallas on the sofa. Passing one to her, he reached his arm around her and snugged her up close. As he gently kissed her temple, he said, "You make me happy." And she did. Happier than any woman had in a very long time. He would have her. That's why he must tread carefully. She had feelings for her cowboy. He had to reel her in, despite those feelings, and make her choose him whole-heartedly.

Leaning her head against his shoulder, she replied, "Ethan, I feel so safe with you. I relax, and you take care of everything. You make the most amazing things happen in my life."

He took Dallas's glass and set it on the table. Tilting her chin, he kissed her, keeping it chaste, warming her slowly to him. His hand grazed her breast as he clasped her waist and turned her toward him. Sliding his fingers into her hair, he deepened the kiss, flicking her lips with his tongue and finally entering her mouth.

Sighing, she relaxed into him, her hand at his cheek, matching him kiss for kiss.

His mouth wandered from hers, tracing the contour of her throat as his hand slipped to her breast, partially exposed by the beautiful gown. Cupping it, his thumb found her swollen nipple and caressed it.

She sucked in a breath.

Returning to her mouth, he delivered a blistering kiss as he cupped her breast, molding it to his hand.

She slid her hand behind his neck, sucking on his tongue, drowning him with hot, hungry kisses.

He pulled back on his mental reins, fighting his own reaction. Now was not the time to lose control. She was where he wanted her now. Desiring him—desperately. But she couldn't have him. Not yet. Not until he overpowered her feelings for that cowboy. When he took her, he'd be the only man she wanted.

Drawing back, he held her face in his hands, holding her gaze. "How lovely you are, Dallas. And what an incredibly lucky man I am to have your affection. But I can't let this go on. You must decide who you love. I know the kind of woman you are, and I won't take advantage." He drew her into a hug. That had come out just right. He was quite proud of himself.

"Thank you, Ethan. You always take care of me. How could I not love you? I've never been so confused in my life."

He set her away from him again. "I know, love, but you have to decide soon. I've fallen for you. I'll do anything to make you mine. Just tell me what you want."

She caressed his face, stroking his cheek with her thumb. "Thank you for caring for me, Ethan, and I'm so sorry to keep you hanging. I'll figure this out. I promise."

Helping her to her feet, he gave her a chaste kiss on the forehead. His plan was proceeding well. Without doubt, Dallas Royle would soon be in his bed, and—not long after—she would be his wife.

* * *

The next day, the limo sat at a stoplight. Dallas smoothed the material of her dress and straightened her bracelet. When Ethan had called last week and told her that his mother had invited them to lunch at her country club, Dallas had almost lost her dinner. The thought of sitting down to another meal with the woman had her trembling, and she hated that. But she was strong and could take anything his mother could dish out. With a deep breath, she crossed her legs and forced her face into a calm mask. She *would* get through this, and nothing Linda said could change how she felt about Ethan.

The big car purred into motion, and Ethan clasped her hand. "I grew up at the club, but I seldom visit anymore. They've remodeled, and it's quite fancy now. Mother and her hens love the new look."

Dallas laughed. "Her hens, huh?"

"Yes, they gather there a couple of afternoons a week and cluck away, always about someone else's business."

She grinned and squeezed his hand. "How lovely."

She hoped her clothing fit in. With no idea what "club ladies" wore, she'd shopped for hours for clothes for this trip and spent her Miscellaneous budget category for the next four months. Her tailored dress in bright summer colors was fashionable without being flashy. No matter what anyone else would be wearing, she felt confident.

As the car slowed to turn down the long drive, she tightened her grip on Ethan's hand. Despite how Linda might behave, he would be there in the chair next to her. Dallas kissed his cheek. "That's for luck. I have a feeling I'm going to need it."

Laughing, he squeezed her fingers. "Will not. We won't stay long, anyway. I'm sure you want to get home to your little girl, Mommy."

She grinned. "I do. Thanks, Ethan, for understanding me."

He dropped a swift kiss on her lips as they pulled up to the entrance.

Dallas eyed the building, with its high asymmetrical walls of glass and chic fountains. Her heartbeat picked up, and her breathing quickened. Putting a hand to her chest, she willed herself to calm down. She would *not* let this woman get to her.

The driver opened her door, and she stepped out.

Ethan followed her. He tucked her hand at his elbow and led her to the door. Pausing, he gave her a quick kiss. "I've got you."

She took a deep breath and nodded. "Let's go."

At the main dining room, he paused, scanning for his mother.

No wonder Linda and her cronies liked the place. The sleek, modern furniture and beautiful garden views from the massive windows gave the room a vibe that said money with a capital *M*. Despite her earlier bravado, Dallas felt smaller, her confidence dwindling.

Ethan led her across the room half-filled with dining members to the table where his mother presided.

Linda had eyes only for her son. Standing for a hug and kiss, she said, "I don't know why you had to stay in that hotel. You're welcome at the house. Separate bedrooms, of course."

"Mother, we have separate bedrooms at the hotel."

Now she turned her gaze to Dallas. "Yes, but do you use them?"

Ethan stepped back, and put his arm around Dallas. "I'll not allow a repeat performance of our last meal with you, Mother. We'll leave now if that's what you're planning."

Linda widened her eyes in alarm. "No, no. Please, we're going to have a pleasant lunch. Chef and I have something wonderful planned, and you're both going to love it." She waved them into their chairs and sat herself.

Dallas kept her eyes on Ethan and away from the gaze of the woman across from her, a look that she knew would turn steely as soon as her son turned his back.

He caught the attention of a waiter and ordered wine.

Linda asked, "How was the symphony, son?" Her eyes clung to Ethan.

Reaching for Dallas's hand, he said, "I've never seen anyone enjoy it more than Dallas did last night. Experiencing the music with her enhanced my enjoyment of the evening."

Linda took a long swallow of her Manhattan and looked out the window. "How nice." After another sip, she turned to Ethan. "The next board meeting is coming up in a few weeks. Did you receive the letter?"

Dallas took a sip of wine. There was an undertone to Linda's voice. What was she after?

Though Ethan hadn't taken the reins of the company as his dad had planned for him, he did accept a seat on the board. He always made sure he knew what was going on with the family business. "I'm planning to attend. I always do."

Linda picked at a fold in her napkin. "You remember Melinda? Her daughter, Tiffany, will be in town from Boston that weekend, and Melinda's invited us to dinner." She smiled brightly. "Please say you'll come. You haven't seen Tiffany in years. She's dying to see you again."

Ethan's mouth tightened into a grim line. "I'll be returning home directly after the board meeting, and you can give Melinda my apologies. I won't be seeing Tiffany or any more of your cronies' daughters. Is that clear enough for you, Mother?"

She huffed and turned to the window. "Quite clear."

Dallas sucked in her bottom lip to hide a smile. It was hard to determine Linda's expression. She'd been given so many Botox injections that her face appeared frozen in the same expression no matter what she felt.

A woman Linda's age walked toward their table. Dallas compared her own outfit to what the other diners were wearing and smiled a little. She'd made a perfect choice. Instead of passing them by, the woman stopped and patted Linda's arm to get her attention. "Hey, honey, I didn't know you'd be here today."

Linda gave the woman a hug and an air kiss. Nodding toward her son, she said, "Of course you remember Ethan."

Then she turned her gaze and frozen smile on Dallas. "Helen, this is the woman I was telling you about. Dallas, this is my good friend, Helen."

Dallas stood and held out her hand.

Helen stared at Dallas, sweeping her hawk-like gaze from top to bottom, then reached out her hand for a genteel shake. "Nice meeting you."

Her tone, however, said it was anything but nice.

"You, too, Helen," Dallas replied in a friendly voice, and sat down.

By the time Linda's fourth friend had stopped by the table, Dallas had figured it out. It was a parade of homes, and she was the model house. None of the women were welcoming, and each one had heard of Dallas. She was sure lunch had been planned at the club so that all of Linda's besties could take a gander at the money-hungry woman Ethan was dating.

Although lunch was probably delicious, she hardly took a bite. Despite Linda's intent gaze, there was nothing Dallas could do about her spasming throat and stomach.

When she declined dessert, Ethan did too. Laying his napkin down, he stood and pushed back his chair. "Mother, we need to get back. I've got a lot to catch up on before court in the morning."

Dallas swept to her feet and grabbed her purse. *Please, God, get me out of this room.*

Linda frowned. "So soon? Can't you stay for another glass of wine?"

Ethan gave her a peck on the cheek. "I'm sorry, Mother. We have to go."

He must have sensed how uncomfortable she was. Thank goodness. She leaned her head against his shoulder as they walked to the door. "Thank you, thank you, a million times, thank you for taking me home."

"I hear you. Sometimes I feel like Mother and her friends suck the life right out of me."

Dallas kept her mouth shut. His mother *was* kind of like a vampire. An evil one, not like the ones in *Twilight.*

The limo was waiting outside, and the driver opened the door as they walked up.

Ethan got in and reached for her hand, helping her scoot close to him. "Come here, sweetheart. Lean on me and relax." He found some classical piano on the radio and turned it down low.

Dallas snuggled her head on his chest and slid her arm across his waist. For the first time that afternoon, she felt completely safe.

As the city traffic thinned and they headed out on the highway, Ethan stroked her arm, kissing her softly on the temple.

She couldn't settle down, though. Lunch had been so upsetting. Her thoughts coalesced into a strong determination. She would never go through an experience like that again. It was time to stand up for herself.

Sitting up straight, she pushed her hair out of her face.

Ethan asked, "Would you like something to drink?"

She didn't want to hurt him, but she had no choice. His mother had made this decision for her. "Not now. Ethan, I need to talk to you."

He frowned. "Is there something wrong?"

"Yes." She clasped his hand, gripping it firmly. "I can't go through another day like today with your mother. I'll be frank. I think she planned lunch at the club so that all her friends could get a good look at me. If you'll remember, when I met each one, she said she'd heard of me. I'm sure your mother said unkind things about me, and they couldn't wait to see the gold digger who had her claws in Linda's only son.

"Your mother ignored me unless she was introducing me. Her smile never reached her eyes. And how about throwing Tiffany at you right in front of me? Ethan, she doesn't like me, she doesn't want me to be part of her family, and she will do anything in her power to come between us. Please, try to understand where I'm coming from."

He pulled her in and hugged her in a tight embrace. "Dallas, you're right. I should have known something was up. Usually those old hags are all over me, and this time they didn't give me a second glance. I swear to God, my mother has sunk to a new low. And how dare she speak ill of you?" Tilting her chin, he kissed her hard, making it last. "Don't you worry. I'll handle this right now."

He grabbed his phone and dialed, crushing it to his ear. "Hello, Mother." He paused to listen for a moment. "No, of course not. We're still driving. I have something to discuss with you, and please don't interrupt. I know what you were up to this afternoon. You made Dallas feel unwelcome and reviled. It will never happen again. The reason I know this is that we won't be seeing you again. You've forced me to make a choice, Mother, and I choose Dallas. There may come a time, in the distant future, when I give you a chance to prove that you not only accept Dallas, but will be kind and caring to her. However, I can't promise that. You're on your own now, Mother. Goodbye."

Terminating the call, he slipped his phone into his pocket and tilted Dallas's face to him. "Nothing—and no one—is more important to me than you, Dallas. My mother will learn that or she'll lose me."

Knowing how much his mother meant to him, Dallas was unable to find words to express her feelings. She clasped his face in her hands and kissed him tenderly. No man had ever sacrificed so much for her. "Ethan, I'm sorry. I know how you love her."

He started to speak, and she shushed him with her fingertips.

She kissed him again. "You've given me a precious gift." This man would give anything, do anything, for her. How could she not love him?

Chapter Thirteen

Monday night, Dallas rocked Piper to sleep. Her daughter had been extra clingy since Sunday evening when Dallas had returned from her trip. Though Piper had enjoyed her time with the nanny and loved her grandparents, she didn't like being away from her mother for so long. After cuddling her daughter a few minutes longer, Dallas at last tucked her in bed and pulled her door nearly shut.

As she poured herself a glass of wine, Dallas's thoughts turned to Ethan and the sacrifice he'd made. A warm rush swept through her. It was still hard to believe that the man had cut his mother from his life to protect Dallas. He'd said that he'd fallen for her. Did that mean he loved her?

She smiled and remembered the feeling of him holding her on the ride home. Never had she been so carefree or content with her life. Ethan handled everything when she was with him, and, despite the fact that she'd always prided herself on her strength and independence, she found that she didn't mind him taking charge.

And, Lord, how the man could kiss. Goose bumps traveled up her arms. He'd thoroughly aroused her. Though she hadn't exactly lost control, she'd reveled in his seduction. Even more, she trusted herself with him. Ethan was a gentleman. But did she love him?

In the darkened living room, she settled on the couch and took a sip of wine, staring at the moonlight coming through the window, mesmerized by the soft shadows it created in the room. In the silent house, she relaxed for the first time since returning home. Leaning her cool glass against her brow, she closed her eyes.

Her phone rang, startling her, and she looked at the display. *Cash.* She hesitated at a pang in her heart. *Am I feeling disloyal to Ethan? Oh, hell!* Accepting the call, she said, "Hey, how are you?"

Ignoring her question, he said, "Dallas? I need to see you. It's important. I'm sorry, I know you just got back from your weekend, but can you get away tomorrow night?"

She swallowed. His voice told her something wasn't right. "Cash, is everything okay?"

"I'm not sure. So what do you think? Can you come?"

Her pulse quickening, she answered. "If it's important, of course I will."

He expelled a loud breath. "Good. I'll pick you up at seven."

She laid her phone down, her hand at her throat. He didn't know if anything was wrong? What did that mean? And where had that fleeting sense of being untrue come from?

It had taken only the sound of Cash's voice to remind her how deeply she cared for him. Groaning, she hid her face in her hands. Her life was on the road to disaster, and she had no idea which path to take.

* * *

Cash laid his phone on the coffee table in the family room and stared at nothing. Hoping Dallas would agree to his request, he'd made reservations at the Salt and Pepper restaurant, the most romantic place in Wichita Falls. He'd also ordered a large bouquet of flowers for pickup on the way to her house and had a small present for Piper that Dallas could give her the next morning. His plan was set.

The past weekend had been awful. Knowing Dallas was with the lawyer made every minute scald his nerves. He'd imagined the man with his arms around her, kissing her, and he'd had to jump in his truck and drive like hell—anything to shove the thoughts away. He didn't know how to keep on going. How to love her and let her be with this man. What he did know was that he was near the limit of what he could take.

* * *

Cash arrived at Dallas's house at straight-up seven. Acid ate at the lining of his stomach. He glanced at the vase of blooms buckled into the passenger seat. Were they too much? Should he have bought a smaller arrangement? Blowing out a few quick breaths, he scrubbed his palms together. He had this. Having practiced what he wanted to say tonight many times, he was sure he'd remember it. Throwing his door open, he strode to the other side of the truck and grabbed the flowers and Piper's gift.

When Dallas answered his knock, his jaw dropped. She was barefoot and fiddling with the back of her earring, but that wasn't what captured his attention. The tight-fitting bodice of her brilliant blue dress pushed her breasts into soft half-moons above the neckline. The garment's slightly clinging material hugged every sensuous curve of her waist and hips. His fingers flexed instinctively. *Lord, how I want this woman.*

Dallas's eyes widened. "Oh, Cash, the flowers are gorgeous. Thank you. Come in." Taking the vase from him, she walked into the living room and placed it on the coffee table. Leaning in, she sniffed a lily. "This smell will fill the entire room. They're wonderful."

He relaxed a little. "I'm glad you like them, Dallas." Clasping her hand, he tugged her gently toward him.

Holding her gaze to the last, he kissed her tenderly. "Thanks for seeing me. I know Piper must have missed you last weekend and how that bothers you."

"She's kind of clingy, for sure. There have been a lot of new things for her to get used to lately."

"I understand. I'm one of them."

Smiling, she said, "That little girl adores you."

The sudden pang in his heart had nothing to do with Dallas. He loved Piper. The fact that she might never be part of his life tore at him. "The feeling's mutual." Handing her the gift, he said, "I got her a little something."

Dallas smiled, and kissed his cheek. "Thank you for thinking of her. Let me get my shoes, and I'll be ready."

They arrived at the restaurant in plenty of time for their reservation. As Cash had anticipated, the candlelit tables created the perfect intimate ambiance for the evening. Once they were seated, he handed Dallas the wine list. "Why don't you choose what you like?"

She smiled at him, an unreadable expression on her face. "Thank you. I'd like that." After finding what she wanted, she ordered.

Dallas glanced around the shadowed dining room. "This place is lovely. I haven't been here before."

"I've eaten here once. I remembered that you said you liked fish, and they're known for their fresh selection here. I was sure you'd like it." He couldn't stop looking at her. It wasn't just that she was beautiful. Dallas shone with goodness, emanating a clean wholesomeness that couldn't be faked. He'd found a woman who embodied everything he wanted in a life partner, and yet, there was the lawyer. The big boogeyman in the equation. He had to find a way to x him out of the equation.

They'd ordered dinner, though now Cash couldn't remember his choice. His focus kept straying to the end of the evening. He rubbed his hands down the thighs of his sharply pressed Wranglers. How would Dallas react?

She took a sip of wine. "What's going on at the ranch?"

"I did some late branding on a bunch of calves out at Rule on Saturday. They were pretty big, and it turned into a rodeo. Other than that, I fed and worked around the homeplace."

"I'd like to see you branding calves sometime."

He reached across the table and clasped her hand. "I'm sure we can make that happen. But enough about me. I want to hear more about you."

Her eyes sparkled in the candlelight. Dallas was funny and easy to talk to, and she kept up a lively conversation.

She laid her napkin on her lap as their food arrived. "You're spoiling me, Cash. How can I go back to macaroni and cheese after a dinner like this?"

"I feel ya. I don't eat like this either."

During the meal, he focused on enjoying his sea bass, preventing the end of the evening from niggling at his pleasure.

When Dallas had eaten as much as she wanted and laid down her fork, he asked, "Would you like dessert?"

"Lord, no. There's no room for it. But thank you."

He caught the attention of their waitress and asked for the check.

As he drove Dallas home, his pulse sped faster with each mile they gained toward her house. He clasped her hand and held on. He'd never been this uncertain in his life, but he couldn't wait any longer.

When they arrived, he parked at the curb and went around to open her door. She took his outstretched hand and stepped out, smiling at him. If only he could frame that look and keep it in his heart.

As they walked to the house, she leaned into his shoulder. "Cash, this was such a special evening."

"I enjoyed it, too." Would it still be special ten minutes from now? He took her keys and opened the door.

"Can you come in, or do you need to go home?"

Thank God. That had been the only thing he couldn't plan. "I'd love to."

She stepped inside. "Would you like a glass of wine?"

"I'm good." He followed her into the living room.

"Me, too. I can't believe how stuffed I am."

Before she could sit, he caught her hand. "Can I have a moment first?"

Raising her brows, she said, "Um, sure."

She'd worn her hair loose tonight, and he loved it that way. He picked up a lock and held it between his fingers. It was so soft. And he was stalling.

He met her gaze, letting her read him, opening up his soul. Now that the time had come, he felt calm, sure of himself. Clasping her hands, he said, "Dallas, meeting you was the best moment of my life. You're the first person I think of when I wake up, and the last one I think of when I go to sleep." He raised her hands to his lips, and kissed them. "Every day, I realize how lucky I am to know you and Piper. I love you, Dallas."

Her pupils dilated, and she sucked in a breath.

He pulled her closer. "I may not be the richest man in the world, but I guarantee you that no amount of riches will be able to buy the amount of love I have for you." Caressing her face, he said, "I'll love you forever, to the last day of my life. You're the woman I want to marry, Dallas. I want you to decide on me."

He'd said what he had to say and said it well.

Dallas's eyes filled with tears and she reached for him. "Cash, I don't deserve you." Her lips trembled. "I don't know what to say. When I'm with you, I love you. I miss you so much when we're apart." She rubbed her forehead on his chest. "I'm a mess. How can I love you like this, and then feel the way I do about Ethan?"

His heart wrenched. She what? Loved *him* but felt—how the hell *did* she feel about the lawyer? *Dammit!*

He slid his fingers into her hair, claiming her mouth with a savage kiss. Every ounce of his frustration went into it. He kissed her again and again, demanding her response. Their tongues fought a silent battle. Grabbing her hips, he ground her against him.

She clung to his neck, hooking him with her leg, pressing her body into him.

Her kisses were like fire, burning his self-control. He trailed his lips down her throat and across the luscious mounds of her breasts.

She moaned and rose up to him.

This woman was his, by God, and nobody else's. He picked her up and held her at his waist.

Wrapping her legs around him, she pulled him down, raining hot, wet kisses on his mouth.

Honor knocked at his consciousness. Reluctantly, he listened. He let her slip slowly to the floor, and held her face in his hands. "I love you, Dallas. You don't have to make your decision tonight. I know you're still confused. You don't have to decide tomorrow, either. But very soon I'll have had all I can take. I love you more than I've ever loved anyone, and it hurts me too bad knowing you're with him. It has to stop, one way or another."

Dallas, still breathing fast, nodded. "It's only fair. I've hurt you, and I don't want to do that anymore. I'll decide." She held him. "Thank you, Cash. For loving me. For everything."

He hugged her hard and headed for the door. He'd done everything he could. He hoped it was enough.

* * *

Wednesday morning, after a restless night, Dallas strained to focus on the document she was preparing. It had to be filed before end of day. She glanced up as Ethan stopped by. He'd been out of the office the past two days. The man looked perfectly groomed, as always. She stopped typing. "Hi, how was court?"

He perched on her desk. "Court was fine, but otherwise I've been terrible. I missed you."

She smiled. "So sorry I ruined things for you."

Picking up a pen, he twirled it in his fingers. "I wanted to remind you that we go to New York in fifteen days."

Crap, really? "Ethan, about that. I was thinking. It's so soon after our Dallas trip, and Piper is pretty clingy right now. I shouldn't go." Cash had monopolized her thoughts since he'd left last night.

Ethan frowned, and she could tell he was annoyed. Maybe even angry. "Dallas, those tickets are incredibly hard to come by, and I've made all the reservations. I won't let you back out now."

Why didn't he understand? Piper needed her too. "This is embarrassing, but I maxed out my budget buying clothes for the symphony trip. I can't afford to go to New York."

His frown disappeared. "I should have realized that. I know a wonderful shop. I'll take you there. My treat."

Her jaw dropped, and she pulled her hand away. "Absolutely *not*. Thank you, Ethan, but that isn't necessary."

Reaching for her hand again, he held it firmly. "It is necessary if that's what's keeping you from accompanying me. I won't take no for an answer, Dallas. I'm making an appointment, and you'll come with me."

His smile didn't quite reach his eyes. He was seriously insisting that she go. The unpleasant incident when he'd spoken so unkindly to his assistant ran through her mind. If she backed out of the New York trip now, would it affect her work? This was an Ethan she didn't recognize.

Removing her hand from his grasp, she squared a stack of papers. She couldn't afford to lose this job.

He tilted his head to catch her gaze.

The old Ethan was back in his infectious smile. "Come on. Say yes."

At least his mother wouldn't be in New York. "Okay, and thank you. But I'll be spending my time with Piper between now and then." After all, she had agreed to go. Fair was fair.

He squeezed her hand, and grinned. "Deal."

She watched his receding back as he headed toward his office. No damned wonder he was so good with juries. The man could sell snow cones on a glacier.

#

That night, after getting Piper to sleep, she called Sarah. It had been too late the previous night after Cash had left. She took a sip of wine as she waited for her friend to answer. "Sarah? Kids in bed? Do you have time to talk?"

"It's Tom's turn to put them down, and he's not doing so well, but I'm all yours. Speak, girl, while I get something to drink."

What would I do without her? "Last night I went out with Cash, and I can't describe how wonderful he was." She told her about their romantic dinner. "Sarah, when we got home, he told me that he loves me. But he didn't just *say* he loves me. He told me in so many ways. It was beautiful."

Pausing, she took another swallow of wine, then continued in a soft voice. "And I love him too. I know that now. For so long I tried to figure out my feelings for Ethan and Cash. I hardly slept last night, and I realized something. There are different kinds of love. One love may fill in my gaps and make me feel whole. Another love may inspire me to be the best I can be. Love can be the thing that brings me pure joy. I have to choose the kind of love I want. Find the man who can give me that."

"Uh-huh. So true, honey."

"Ethan's love fills in my gaps. He's like a safety net. I'll never want financially when I'm with him, and he takes charge of everything when we're together. I'm never that scared little girl when I'm with him. I feel safe and loved and content."

"What about Cash?"

"His love is simple and kind and accepting. Cash understands me when I least expect it. He's patient and slow to anger. His love is the type that can last a lifetime. He makes me happy."

"I think you have your answer, girl," Sarah said.

"I do, don't I?"

Sarah gave a short laugh, "I don't envy you. Now it's time to do something about it."

Her heart sank. It was a mess. She couldn't tell Cash how she felt. Not with this trip to New York ahead of her. How would that look? If only Ethan hadn't insisted she go.

Ending the call and tossing her phone on the cushion beside her, she took a long draught of wine. Ethan had seemed almost sinister today when she'd tried to back out of going. She'd never seen that side of him before, but she knew she hadn't imagined it. Why was her going so important to him? It couldn't just be the money. She forced the muscles in her abdomen to relax. She'd get through this trip and have a pleasant time while preserving her working relationship with him. Then she could tell Cash—and Ethan—her choice.

* * *

Dallas reclined on the couch late Sunday evening, fiddling with the stem of her wine-glass. She missed Cash. He understood her need to spend her time off with Piper this week, but his absence had left her feeling surprisingly lonely.

It would be wonderful to hear his voice, but conflicting feelings warred inside her. Despite her misgivings, she'd agreed to go to New York. That put sharing her final decision over two weeks away. Somehow, when Cash had said that he'd wait a little while longer, she didn't think he meant that long.

Her phone rang. It was Cash. The decision to call him had been taken from her, and she smiled as she lifted it to her ear. "Hi."

"Hey." He yawned quietly. "Excuse me. I figured Piper would be asleep by now."

"She is. I'm glad you called. I was just thinking about you." Hearing his deep voice set off butterflies in her tummy.

"Really?"

"Yeah... Listen, what you said the other night. It was beautiful." God, had it been beautiful.

"I meant every word of it."

"I know. That's what made it wonderful." She had to do it. It was wrong having this conversation without telling him.

"Cash?"

"Hmm?"

"Ethan made these plans a long time ago, and I tried to get out of it, but he said the tickets were very expensive, and he won't let me back out now." It was dumb, but her hands shook and it was getting hard to breathe. How would Cash react?

He didn't say anything.

"Cash?"

"What tickets?"

"To a Broadway play in New York. It's in eleven days. We'd leave on Thursday evening and come back Sunday after lunch. "

His silence stretched on for several moments.

When she couldn't stand it any longer, she said, "I'm sorry, Cash. He's a partner at the firm. I got this feeling—"

His voice shaking, he said, "Wait." Dead silence followed.

Something was happening with him, and it terrified her. She set her wine on the table, then knocked it over. *Dammit!* Would the red wine ruin the pale wood?

Cash heaved out a loud breath and, with his voice still shaking, said, "You know that I love you, and you know how much. I want to hang in there for you, but I... Dallas, I just can't. Not for this." He took another rasping breath, and said in a strangled voice, "I don't want to lose you, but you've made your choice. I have to let you go." The line went dead.

Stunned, heart pounding, she lurched from her seat, pacing the room. With trembling fingers, she dialed him back.

It went to his voicemail.

Shaking and cold, she stumbled to the couch and called him again.

He didn't answer.

Frantic, she phoned Sarah. As soon as her friend answered, Dallas, sobbing, spilled the whole story.

When Dallas ran out of words, Sarah said, "Honey, I know you're heartbroken."

She wiped her nose with the back of her hand. "I had to be truthful to him. I'm not sorry." Cash deserved to know.

"No, you did right."

"Oh, Sarah, what am I going to do?" This devastation reminded her of when Piper's father had walked out on her.

"I don't have the answer, hon. You have to figure this one out for yourself."

The fact was that there was nothing to figure out. Cash had turned his back on her.

Chapter Fourteen

Cash took his beer and change and stepped away from the bar. The band rocked the house as the bass player riffed madly, nearly piercing Cash's eardrum. Jesse and Boone had brought him to The Longhorn Saloon in Wichita Falls, hoping to take his mind off his breakup with Dallas. So far, it wasn't working.

Jesse met him as he approached their table. He slung his arm across Cash's shoulders. "Come on, bud, don't be a lightweight. That's only your third beer. We're here to get *drunk!* At least you and Boone are. I'm driving."

His friend was right. Cash threw his head back and chugged his entire bottle.

Jesse laughed. "Now that's more like it. Come on, I have someone I want you to meet."

Jesse walked ahead of him to the table, calling out, "He needs another beer, Boone."

"I'm on it." Boone grinned and slapped Cash's back on the way to the bar.

Jesse looked around. "I'll be right back."

Cash shook his head in resignation. Between his two best friends, he had no chance of staying sober tonight. But what the hell. He'd be miserable sober or drunk, so he might as well drink. He missed Dallas so badly that he found it hard to eat or sleep. And work? That was a joke. It seemed that all he did was mess things up.

Just then, Jesse showed back up, pulling a good-looking, dark-haired woman in his wake. With a flourish, he said,

"Tanya, this is my friend, Cash." He winked. "I'm dating her best friend, so you'd better take good care of her."

Tanya raised her eyebrows and grinned. "Nice to meet you, Cash. Don't listen to him. I can take care of myself."

Damn. Though partying and dancing with other women had been part of the plan for the night, now that the time had come, he had no heart for it.

The band started up a two-step. Jesse grabbed a girl and slapped Cash on the back. "Come on, bro, get out there."

Tanya looked at him with a grin, waiting for him to ask her out on the floor.

Dallas was lost to him. He had to get used to that fact. This was as good a way as any to start. Holding out his hand, he said, "Would you do me the honor, Tanya?"

She was a great dancer. No matter what he asked of her, she spun, turned, and scooted at his bidding. If she were Dallas, he'd have loved dancing with her. As it was, he couldn't wait for the song to end. It didn't feel right having another woman in his arms when all he wanted was to hold Dallas tight and kiss her until he drove all thoughts of that lawyer from her mind.

The music stopped, and he led Tanya from the floor. When they got to the table, he held her hand for a moment longer. "I need to tell you something. Being here tonight is what Boone and Jesse cooked up because I've been in a funk lately. I'm sorry, but I don't feel much like talking or dancing. I don't want to keep you from having fun. Will you excuse me?"

Her gaze softened. "It's okay, Cash. I understand." She headed off down the row of tables.

Jesse and his girl walked by a few seconds later. "Where's Tanya?"

Cash held up his finger. "No more dancing partners. I'm sitting here and drinking in peace, buddy."

Jesse frowned. "But—"

"No buts. Quit fixing me up."

Jesse nodded and studied him for a bit. "You got it, bro. Holler when you want another beer."

Half of his buddies' solution worked. By the time they headed home, Cash wasn't thinking of Dallas. He wasn't thinking of anything. The next morning, he couldn't remember leaving the bar, arriving home, or getting into bed. His buddies had taken care of those things for him.

* * *

The gentle clip-clop of the horse's hooves lulled Dallas's jangled senses—a case of nerves caused by this three-day trip to New York with Ethan when her heart ached for Cash. For their first night, Ethan had suggested a carriage ride through Central Park, and he'd made dinner reservations at a restaurant in Tribeca.

On the ride to the airport that morning, she'd told Ethan that Cash had broken up with her. Ethan was obviously pleased, although he'd been sympathetic about her loss. She squeezed her eyes shut. She had to get over it—forget about Cash. Ethan was all she had now. Why wasn't she ecstatic over this trip to the Big Apple? She just wasn't trying hard enough. "This is beautiful. I didn't know the park was so big."

Pulling her tighter against his side, Ethan said, "The best way to see Central Park is by carriage ride."

Leaning her head on his shoulder, she reached for that peaceful, secure sensation he always gave her.

He kissed her forehead, resting his cheek against her.

Her chest eased a little as she watched the horse's rump sway side-to-side in rhythm with the sound of its hooves. Mesmerized, her mind calmed. Maybe this trip was what she needed.

A town car waited for them as they stepped down from the carriage.

Ethan caught her hand and whisked her to the door, which their driver held open. "We've just enough time to make our reservations." Once inside the car, he tilted her chin and kissed her gently. "I'm so happy you're here with me. I can't wait to show you New York."

Looking into his eyes, it was clear how much he meant it. But where was her own enthusiasm? A deep sadness weighed down her heart, and she couldn't seem to escape it. "I'm looking forward to it."

Ethan kept her entertained during dinner with vacation-gone-wrong stories. By the time they were back in the car, she was in a cheery mood. As they pulled up to the majestic entrance of the New York Palace Hotel, she marveled again at its old-world beauty. Inside were gilded balustrades, frescoed ceilings, and tall columns. Their two-bedroom suite, elegant in every detail, had a gorgeous view of historic St. Patrick's Cathedral. Ethan had gone way over the top in his effort to make her happy.

Once at their rooms, he opened the door and ushered her inside. "Have a glass of wine with me?"

She smiled, yet shook her head. "Can we not, tonight? It's been such a long day. All I can think of is my pillow." The day's anxiety had drawn on every last bit of reserve energy she had.

Ethan tossed his room key on the end table. "At least give me a proper goodnight, then." He grinned and drew her to him. Clasping her hands, he pulled them behind her back and kissed her thoroughly.

His kiss left her oddly unmoved. Her pulse didn't race, her breath didn't quicken. A man had never kissed her in that strangely vulnerable position, and she didn't like it.

Ethan brushed her cheek with his fingertips, and released her. "Sleep in a while in the morning. Why don't we eat in the room and leave here around eleven?"

"I'll see you tomorrow." She couldn't get to her bedroom fast enough. As she showered and prepared for bed, her anxiety returned. Why hadn't her body responded to Ethan's kiss? She'd always loved how he kissed—the man was amazing at it. Yet she might as well have been made of stone just now. Ethan cared for her—spared no expense where she was concerned, left no detail unplanned. As a provider, he could make her the happiest woman in the world.

She slid into the cold sheets and turned off the lamp. Cash was no longer a part of her life. Now she might lose Ethan too. She couldn't spend her life with a man who left her physically unmoved. Sweat moistened her palms, and she rubbed them absently on the duvet. Cash's loss had upended her world, and she was still struggling to find peace with it. Could that be her problem? She just needed time to pull herself together, and then she would respond to Ethan as she had in the past? Sighing deeply, she turned on her side. Surely her old self would be back in no time.

* * *

The next evening, Dallas slipped her feet into the four-inch heels that matched the outfit Ethan had picked out for her when they went shopping. The knee-length black dress was snug with off-the-shoulder cap sleeves and a deep V neckline.

Earlier in the day he'd taken her to Little Italy, Chinatown, and Times Square, and she'd seen the Statue of Liberty from across the bay.

She met him in the living room, where he was taking in the view of the cathedral. "All ready."

He strode to her, pulling her in for a quick kiss. "You're gorgeous." Stepping back, he eyed her up and down. "My God, look at you. I'm a lucky man."

Grinning, she said, "You're pretty spectacular yourself." His elegant, perfectly fitted black suit made them a striking pair.

As he opened the door, he said, "I made dinner reservations, too."

His smile hinted at something special, and it piqued her curiosity. Clasping his arm, she walked proudly at his side, headed for her first Broadway show.

* * *

Dallas clapped as the cast bowed for the last time. The musical had been everything she'd hoped for. And, in true Ethan style, their seats had been perfect—in the center, third row from the stage, in the orchestra section. She tightened her wrap as he helped her to her feet.

He put his hand at her waist as they slowly filed out of the theater.

Glancing at him, she smiled and stepped a little closer as a wave of warmth swept through her. Ethan was so good to her. He had it wrong. She was the lucky one. Continually thinking of ways to make her happy, he was a giving and caring man. Everything was going to be okay.

The limo waited for them, and Ethan pulled her close as she slid inside. He tilted her face to him and kissed her tenderly, yet with the heat of male power.

She kissed him back, pulling him to her, willing her body to respond.

He angled his mouth for a deeper kiss, running his hand up her waist.

She drew back, inching away from him. "So, where are we going for dinner?" The kiss hadn't worked. She'd felt nothing.

He settled back against the seat. "It's something different—in a chef's private home. Reservations are very hard to come by, and he's agreed to stay open a bit later for us tonight." He squeezed her fingers. "I hope you like it."

"I'm sure I will." Closing her eyes, she turned her head away. A few more days were all she needed. Then she'd feel something. She had to.

Ten minutes later, they arrived at the French restaurant and followed the maître d' to their table.

Ethan seated her, and she glanced around the room. Though there were several other tables, they were empty since the place had already closed. The unique aspect of this eatery was the open-plan kitchen, which took up one whole wall of the small dining room. This meant that they could watch the chef and his staff prepare the intricate courses they would be served.

Their wine came, and Ethan told her, "We don't need to order. Chef Charles has a wonderful dinner planned for us tonight."

This fabulous—and surely expensive—evening was so alien to her, yet Ethan seemed in his element. "I don't know what to say. Tonight is out of this world."

"I like making you happy."

She reached across the table, and he clasped her hand. They sat that way for a while, and she was content. Then the first entrée arrived. And the dishes kept coming. She'd heard of places like this. Each plate or bowl held a tiny portion of unique-looking food. She tried it all. Some were fabulous, others were...interesting. Her only clue that the meal had ended was when dessert was served.

Ethan must have noticed her look of relief. He grinned. "You survived. What did you think?"

"Honestly? I really loved most of it. A couple of things, though, I didn't really care for. Did they just pull green stuff out of a field and cut it up?"

He cracked up. "I agree. You'll notice I didn't eat everything, either." Pausing, he reached for her hand. "Dallas, I know I put a lot of pressure on you to come this weekend. I'd planned everything in great detail, and I have to admit I had an ulterior motive. I have something to show you, but don't make your decision just yet." He reached into his pocket and produced a beautifully cut white-gold engagement ring set with a stunning diamond solitaire. "I love you, Dallas, and I want to marry you."

Her heart lurched and began to pound. She grew light-headed. This couldn't be happening. Not yet. Maybe not ever. *Oh, Cash!*

Ethan frowned slightly.

Hell, she must look as terrified as she felt. "Ethan, I—"

Before she could go on, he said, "I don't want you to accept this now, Dallas. There's something else you must do first. The hotel delivered a draft of a prenuptial agreement to your room this evening. I'll pay for an attorney of your choosing to review it with you, and, within reason, we can modify it. Please understand, this isn't anything to do with you personally. I own a large part of my family business, and I have a responsibility to protect those assets."

She gazed at him as her heart slowed and cold seeped in. How very different was Ethan's declaration of love from Cash's baring of his soul. A crushing weight built and built in her chest, making it almost impossible to take a breath.

Ethan closed the ring box and rushed to her. Kneeling, he pulled her into a hug. "I've hurt you, and I never meant that. I'm so sorry, Dallas. I have no choice in this. I wanted you to know about the prenup before you said yes. Though people in the circle I grew up with take a prenup for granted, I knew you might not be expecting one."

She nodded against his chest, feeling absolutely nothing. "I understand, Ethan. Please don't worry."

* * *

The hollowness stayed with her through their flight back to Dallas the next day, and in the limo ride home, and during the kiss Ethan gave her at her front door.

He clung to her a moment longer. "Dallas, please don't turn down my proposal without reading the document. It's extremely generous as prenups go. It's not meant to hurt you in any way."

She pulled back and attempted a smile. "I have so much to think about, not just the prenup, Ethan. I'm confused and tired and completely unable to talk about it right now, okay?"

Kissing her forehead. he whispered, "I understand." With one last look into her eyes, he walked back to the limo.

By the time she'd told her parents a little about the trip and retrieved Piper, she could hardly move. Her daughter wanted Dallas's undivided attention, which she gave the little girl while stretched out on the couch. Thank God Piper could entertain herself. All Dallas had to do was act as her cheering section.

Thoughts roiled inside Dallas's head. Ethan's businesslike proposal. The amazing new experiences they'd shared in New York. How he'd planned down to the tiniest detail to ensure her happiness. And a prenup that would limit the amount of financial security she would achieve in the marriage. It was a document in existence for one reason only—their divorce. Never in her life had she thought of marriage as a purely financial agreement. She considered marriage a matter of loving someone with all your heart. Of course she'd thought of the financial security that Ethan could offer her, but she'd never once considered a future with him without loving him.

She knew someone else who thought of marriage as two people loving each other with all their hearts. But he'd given up on her. She squeezed her eyes shut, the weight in her chest suddenly seeming too much to bear. She turned over and curled up tight. Her stomach churned. Without a bite to eat all day, the burning sensation in her belly grew stronger.

Piper had already eaten dinner, so Dallas only needed to hold it together until her bedtime. She could last that long. Though she seldom used them, tonight she would take two over-the-counter sleeping pills. She couldn't bear a night haunted by a man who no longer cared, a man who had forgotten her. A cowboy she was no longer allowed to love.

Chapter Fifteen

Ethan checked his tie and opened his office door. After spending the past three days in court, he wanted to take Dallas to lunch. Surely she'd called a lawyer by now about the prenup? With the cowboy out of the picture, nothing stood in Ethan's way. He'd just received some wonderful news from the Dallas firm that made moving forward with his plans even more critical.

Dallas was focused intently on her computer screen and didn't notice him until he leaned on her desk.

He smiled at her. "Go to lunch with me? I've missed you."

She frowned. "Ethan, I'd love to, but I'm so behind. I'm still catching up from taking Friday off. Rain check?"

Dallas seemed tired. Her makeup wasn't quite hiding the dark circles under her eyes. Was she that upset over the damn prenup? "Are you okay, Dallas?" This was probably not a good time to ask about the attorney.

She gave him a half-hearted smile. "Fine. Just haven't been sleeping all that well. Must be a full moon."

Hoping to make her laugh, he said, "I thought that only bothered little old ladies." It worked.

"I feel like one today. I'm sorry I can't go, Ethan. Thanks for asking."

Back in his office, he was too restless to settle into reviewing the document his assistant had given him earlier that morning. Dallas occupied his thoughts. The prenup shouldn't prevent her from marrying him. He had so much to offer her. She'd never want for anything. He'd pay for her university, and afterwards, she'd never have to work. Of course, her daughter would go to the very best schools. He'd make sure of it. Her education would prepare her for an Ivy League college. He and Dallas would travel extensively, of course.

So why did he sense an underlying problem? She didn't seem like a woman who'd had a man lay the world at her feet. Sure, there was the matter of the prenup, but he got the feeling that that wasn't the whole problem. Maybe she hadn't thought about all the benefits that marrying him offered.

He picked up his cell and called her. "Would you please come to dinner at my place Sunday evening? It's important. It'll be casual, don't worry."

She hesitated. "It's important?"

"It really is. Please?"

"Of course I'll come."

"I'll send a car. Thank you, Dallas." He had three days to plan. Dallas was the perfect woman for him. Intelligent, inherently good. A fine mother and absolutely gorgeous. Sunday, he'd close this deal.

* * *

Saturday morning, Dallas sat at the kitchen table at her parents' house, drinking coffee with her mother while her daughter watched cartoons in the living room. "Mom, I didn't tell you something that happened on my New York trip. Ethan asked me to marry him."

Her mother's eyes widened, then narrowed as she examined Dallas's face. "Something's wrong."

Dallas sighed and took a drink of her coffee. "Yeah. It is. He gave me a prenuptial agreement to review. The whole thing is weird." She surveyed the cracks on the opposite wall. "That's just part of my problem, if you can believe it. Since Cash broke up with me, I quit feeling or something."

Searching her mom's face, she said, "I remember caring deeply for Ethan, but that's gone. How can I marry him if I don't get that feeling back?"

"You can't, honey."

Her face crumpled. "What's wrong with me, Momma?"

Her mom reached across the table and clasped her wrists, giving her a shake. "Look at me now. One thing I know is there's nothing wrong with you. You're honest and true. It doesn't matter who you marry as long as that man makes you feel whole, and strong, and joyful. That's when you'll have a good life."

Dallas blinked, and sucked in a breath. Whole and strong and joyful. How wonderful would it be to feel like that? "Momma, you're so wise. I love you." She called Piper and picked up her purse. She had a lot of thinking to do.

* * *

Ethan tucked the two bound reports out of sight on top of the refrigerator. After working on them all weekend, he had the perfect presentation ready for Dallas. He uncorked the wine and poured himself a glass. She should arrive any minute. It was hard to believe, but his pulse was racing. So much depended on her response. She *must* see the wisdom in marrying him, and he hoped she would agree to do so tonight.

He heard the car pull up outside and went to the door to meet her. With her long golden hair and wearing the bright summer dress they'd bought when he'd taken her shopping, Dallas looked stunning as she stepped out of the car. God, he absolutely had to make this woman his wife.

Hurrying down the steps, he took her in his arms. "Welcome. I opened the wine, and dinner is ready. I ordered in, and it just arrived."

She smiled and followed him into the house.

Wanting a more intimate setting than the large table where he entertained, he led her to the kitchen and pulled out a chair for her at the table. "I thought we could eat in here. You can get lost in my big dining room."

"Fine with me. This is a beautiful kitchen. Do you cook a lot?"

He glanced around his state-of-the-art kitchen outfitted with stainless steel appliances and stocked with everything a chef could want. "No, not at all. I'm not really into it. If I have guests, I have it catered. Do you cook?"

She grinned. "Uh, not much choice here. I do simple things, mostly. Working two jobs, I don't have much time to cook. My mom taught me some old family recipes that are nice, though."

Pouring her a glass of wine, he said, "You work way too hard."

She sighed. "Again, not much choice. Not if I want to go back to school."

He nodded and headed over to the oven, where he removed four foil trays and set them on a baking sheet. After taking them and a basket of warm bread to the table, he grinned at Dallas. "Lots and lots of Italian food. Dig in."

He kept the conversation light during dinner. His stomach had tied itself in knots, and he wasn't hungry. He nibbled at his food, ready for the damned meal to end.

At last, she set her fork down. "I can't eat another bite. Ethan, the way you feed me, I'm going to get fat."

Laughing, he teased, "Don't you dare!" With a gesture, he said, "Head on into the living room. I'll be right there." As she left the room, he retrieved the reports from their hiding place, grabbed the wine and his glass, then paused, taking a deep breath. This was it. He put on his most engaging smile and strode from the room.

Dallas sat on the sofa sipping her wine. She smiled at him as he approached.

He hoped she would still be smiling when he finished his presentation. Sitting down beside her, he handed her a report.

She read the cover, and her forehead wrinkled. "*Long-term Benefits of Marriage?*"

Nodding, he gave her a paper. "Yes, but before we start, have you reviewed the prenuptial agreement?"

She shook her head. "Ethan, I need to tell—"

"That's okay. I listed three attorneys here who are experienced with them, and they're expecting your call. Now, Dallas, God forbid that something should happen to our marriage, but if it did, you and Piper would be well taken care of. You *must* read the document. Really, marrying me is a win-win situation for you." He opened his report. "Let's look at tab one."

Dallas, her voice strained, said, "Ethan, I need to talk—"

He clasped her hand. "Please, let me go over this with you. Remember I that said tonight was important? This is what I meant. Okay?"

Sucking in her lower lip, she nodded slowly.

"Okay, tab one." She opened her book.

"As you can see, I calculated the cost of your completed legal degree and bar exam. You'll have no living expenses because we'll be married. You'll note that that's quite a substantial amount, which I'm thrilled to pay for you. Now, if you'll turn the page, I did some research, and these worthy organizations would love for you to volunteer your services, pro bono, as your time allows. Of course, after we're married, you'll be accompanying me to social events and raising our young children, so that time will be somewhat limited."

Glancing up, he noticed her jaw had dropped. He rushed to say, "Don't worry, you'll have a nanny."

In a firm voice, she said, "Ethan, I will *not*—"

Holding up his hand, he said, "Dallas, please let me finish. I worked hard on this, and I think you'll agree it's a wonderful proposal by the time I'm done."

She narrowed her eyes, yet kept silent.

"Now, tabs two and three go together. They represent junior and senior boarding schools." Dallas's face had gone completely still. Quickly flipping tab two open, he said, "These pages introduce four outstanding junior boarding schools that accept students starting at kindergarten. Not all junior schools do. I checked their credentials and references, and they're above reproach. An approximate cost for a nine-year education is listed here." He glanced at Dallas. Her hand lay on the unopened tab, and a rosy shade of pink crawled up her exposed chest.

He hurriedly flipped to tab three. She needed to understand the great benefits of having a high-quality education. "The same goes for the boarding schools in the next tab, which start at a student's freshman year. These schools have a between 20% and 30% graduation rate to Ivy League universities."

Dallas's face and ears had turned red. She bit her lip, staring down at the report.

Exhaling sharply, he said, "Dallas, *I* went to boarding schools. It was good for me. I excelled at university, and I'm a successful businessman. All our children should go."

She wouldn't look at him, and his heart dropped. Somehow this had turned out terribly wrong.

He shut the report and set it on the table. Easing the booklet off her lap, he did the same with hers. Clasping her hands, he tilted her face until he could see into her eyes. "I just want to take care of you. The only way I know how."

With her voice shaking, she said, "I'm really trying to understand that." She looked down and seemed to be collecting her thoughts. At last, she sighed and met his gaze. "Ethan, you said you love me. But how you can love me, yet know so little about me, is beyond my understanding."

His heart lurched, pounding his chest wall. *No. No. This can't be happening.* He leaned forward, but before he could speak, she continued.

Shaking her head from side to side, she said, "Do you actually think I'm a woman who would spend years earning a degree to practice law, then not work at the career I've always dreamed of?"

"But I only—"

She talked right over him. "And you've seen me with my daughter. You know how much she means to me. How you *ever* thought that I would send Piper away to boarding school is beyond my comprehension."

She pressed her lips into a grim line. "Ethan, you don't love me. You love some idea of me that you've made up in your head. I can't marry you. We'd never in a million years be happy." She squeezed his hands. "But thank you for caring for me and for trying to make me happy." Standing, she stepped away from the sofa, away from him. "Would you please call the car? I'd like to go home."

He stared, transfixed, as she walked to the front door and then stepped outside. Rubbing the heel of his palm against his chest, he squeezed his eyes shut. *My God, I've lost her.*

Chapter Sixteen

Dallas sat cross-legged in the darkness. It was three thirty in the morning, and she hadn't slept since returning from dinner with Ethan. Though she tried, her muscles tensed, her pulse racing in company with her mind. Rising from the couch, she headed for the kitchen to refill her wineglass. A type of calm had come over her after finishing the first bottle.

Returning to the living room, she settled into the cushions. How had she been so mistaken about Ethan? She'd thought she knew him. She'd met his mother. He'd told her all about himself. Of course there were differences between them, but how had she missed the...the not wanting to raise his own children? It was so fundamentally wrong. At least, according to the way she'd been raised. Yet he'd thought that he was giving Piper a wonderful opportunity. Dallas had assumed that Ethan was more like her, and he'd thought she was more like him.

Her head spun—and not just from the wine. The bricks that had built her happiness had crumbled into dust. Cash was lost to her. Ethan wasn't the man she'd thought he was. Taking a large swallow of wine, she set her glass on the table. Her life sucked, and she had nobody to blame but herself. She'd done nothing but make poor choices since she'd started dating two men at the same time. What kind of dummy thought that situation would work?

She drew her knees up and wrapped her arms around them. Cold seeped into her limbs. Now she was truly alone. This felt different than any aloneness she'd experienced before. Numbness began in her chest and slowly spread through her body.

She couldn't face Ethan. No way could she dwell on Cash. Picking up her phone with unfeeling fingers, she called her boss at work, reaching his office voicemail. "Hi, this is Dallas. I'm so sorry, but I'm sick. I won't be able to come in tomorrow." After making the same call to her other boss at the firm, she lay down, curling in on herself. Change was coming to her life. That much was obvious. But not right now. She clutched her stomach harder. Not tonight.

* * *

Monday morning, Cash yanked on a strand of barbed wire and glanced at his father, who stood a few feet away. They'd been mending fence all morning and Cash wanted to bring up Dallas. His dad knew that he'd been seeing her, but Cash hadn't told him that he'd broken up with her. Instead of missing her less or getting over her, he was a bigger mess now than he'd ever been. "Dad?"

His father looked up from the kinks he was making in the second, sagging strand of wire. "Yeah?"

"Remember I told you about Dallas?"

"Yep, pretty thing. Has a daughter."

"Well, there's something I didn't tell you." He explained about Ethan. Then Cash told him how he'd gotten jealous and broken it off with her.

His dad tested the wire, which was now tight, and turned back to Cash. "Son, seems you're bringing this up for a reason. What is it?"

Cash stared at a small prickly pear growing in the fence line and kicked it loose from the soil with his boot. "I was miserable because she was dating that other guy. I didn't know missing her would be so much worse."

His dad stuck his hands on his hips, chewing the corner of his mouth as he looked Cash up and down. "Do you love her?"

He met his father's gaze and said in a strong voice, "Yes, I do."

His dad shook his head, "Well, damn, boy, I didn't raise you to be a quitter. What the hell are you doing standing here? Go fight for her."

A jolt of excitement hit Cash, replacing the sense of helplessness he'd felt the past couple of weeks. He thought of nothing but Dallas as he and his father gathered their tools and headed for the truck.

* * *

Monday morning, Dallas woke chilled and empty and slightly hung over. She'd fallen asleep in an awkward position, and her neck had a kink in it. Groaning, she sat up and went into the kitchen to make a cup of coffee and a piece of toast. Thank God Piper had slept at her parents' house last night.

Although she felt physically lousy, her mind had cleared. Last night she'd passed through the fog of recrimination and depression that had crushed her in its grip. The late morning sun shone through the window as she returned to the couch. She'd come to a decision. Cash might have turned his back on her, but she wouldn't give up on him. Not without reaching out one more time. Losing Cash had ultimately been her fault. Maybe there was a chance she could make things right again.

The hot coffee warmed her insides as the toast soothed her raw-feeling stomach. She ached to see Cash, to feel his arms around her, to hear his deep voice. She'd lost him without realizing the great treasure she had. That was the saddest part—the part that broke her heart. He'd handed her his soul, and she hadn't valued it for the exquisite gift it was.

Picking up her phone, she paused, took a slow breath for courage, and texted Cash:

If I call you, will you answer?

Immediately, he sent back:

Yes! I was going to call. I want to see you tonight.

Grinning, fingers trembling with excitement, she typed:

I'm off today if you want to come over before then.

Her heart leapt when he sent:

Give me two hours. I'll be there.

She couldn't stop smiling. Every nerve in her body tingled. Cash would be walking through her door soon. God had answered her prayers.

After showering, she slipped into a simple sundress and styled her hair, then tidied the house. By the time two hours had passed, she was checking her phone every couple of minutes, wondering where Cash was. How should she react when he arrived? She wanted to throw her arms around him and kiss him until she ran out of breath. But after what had happened, she couldn't. Or could she?

A brisk knock sounded at her door. Pulse thrumming in anticipation, she smoothed her sundress, then grabbed the door handle and pulled it open. Her heart tumbled in her chest. She caught a quick glimpse of Cash, straw Stetson pulled low on his forehead, before he crushed her to him.

His familiar scent overwhelmed her. His arms were like bands of iron. She felt small and fragile and protected, yet at the same time more like herself than she had in ages.

He stepped back and looked into her eyes. "I'm sorry I didn't answer your calls."

Shaking her head vigorously, she said, "No, I'm sorry. For everything."

She led him to the couch and held his hands as they sat down. "I'd already decided I wanted to marry you. How could I not? And I tried to back out of going to New York. Ethan got angry and was insistent I go. I was afraid it would affect my job if I didn't, so I agreed. I thought I had to do that one thing, since I'd promised, and then I could tell him I'd chosen you, and it would all be over." She squeezed his hands, her eyes imploring. "I'm so sorry I hurt you. I was only thinking of myself. I was so worried about losing my job I put everything else second."

Rubbing her forehead, she said. "My job wasn't in jeopardy at the time. Ethan had made elaborate plans to propose to me on the trip. That's why he put so much pressure on me to go."

Cash stiffened and frowned. "That guy asked you to marry him? So what happened?"

She shook her head. "I said no."

Cash leaned back on the couch, pulling her against his chest. "I was miserable without you. I thought I could handle it, but, no way." He kissed her temple. "I'm glad you got ahold of me, but I would have been calling you in a few minutes, anyway. My dad finally talked some sense into me."

Slipping her arm around his waist, she nestled her head against him. "You were all I could think about. I knew what a terrible mistake I'd made, but I couldn't fix it. You didn't want me anymore."

He tilted her chin so she could see the truth in his face. "I never stopped wanting you. I was stupid to let you go. I should have fought for you instead of giving up." Lowering his mouth to hers, he kissed her tenderly. When he pulled back, he looked into her eyes. "Will you marry me, Dallas?"

Her pulse quickened. "Yes, yes," she breathed, and teased his lips with a kiss.

He hissed in a breath and took control of the kiss, cradling her head in his hand.

She darted her tongue between his lips as he moaned and pulled her into his lap.

She clasped his face and captured his mouth, kissing, sucking, nibbling, feeling every muscle in his body tense.

Holding her waist, he pushed her back sharply. "God, I want you, Dallas." His look was wild, yet so full of love it set her on fire.

She stood and pulled him up beside her. Wrapping her arms around his neck, she kissed him, hard. "I want you, too, cowboy. Follow me."

A shiver ran through her. Cash would be the first man in her bedroom. The first man in her bed. The first man to make love to her since Piper's father had turned his back on her. Joy swelled in her breast. This marvelous man would be her first love all over again.

They stood beside the bed, and he pulled her into his arms, whispering, "I've dreamed of this. Of making love to you. I thought I'd lost you. I was such a fool." He kissed her gently, again and again. He kissed her fingers. "I'll never let you go again, Dallas. I promise."

She rose up on her tiptoes, and kissed him. "Make love to me, Cash." She ached to feel his hands on her, wanted to explore every inch of his hard body.

Grinning, he slipped the straps of her sundress off her shoulders and unzipped the back. "My pleasure, ma'am."

Sliding it down her waist and hips, he knelt as she stepped out of the dress. She stood before him clad only in a tiny pair of panties.

His gaze raked over her body, and she sucked in a breath, her breasts tightening in response.

Standing, he rested his hands at her waist and kissed her. "You're beautiful, Dallas. But that word doesn't come near to describing you."

Intent now, she unbuttoned his shirt, fumbling a little in her hurry. Yanking it out of his Wranglers, she slid it off his shoulders and tossed it on the chair.

Cash pulled her to him and kissed her, nibbling on her neck.

Goose bumps broke out on her arms, making the small hairs stand on end. She ran her hands across the muscles of his broad chest, then dropped them to his waist and hooked her fingers in his jeans, pulling him tight against her.

Cash moaned and grasped her bottom with both hands, yanking her to him, grinding her against him. Then he abruptly let go and took hold of his belt, unbuckling it while toeing a boot off.

She unzipped him while he toed his other boot off.

Kicking his boots away, he yanked down his jeans and briefs and stepped out of them as he reached for her.

Chills ran up and down her body. He was gorgeous, his strong, muscular body molded by strenuous ranch work.

He captured her mouth in a hungry kiss. Grabbing her butt, he pulled her tight, kissing her behind the ear.

She inhaled sharply and drew back. Taking hold of the bedspread and sheet, she dragged them to the end of the bed.

Cash stopped her before she could get in. Slipping his forefingers inside her panties at the hips, he eased them down to the floor.

As she stepped out of them, he kissed her thigh. She quivered. He kissed higher, trailing soft kisses up her belly as her nipples hardened into pebbles. He landed kisses on her collarbone, along the curve of her throat, and released the tiniest breath in her ear. Shivers raced through her body.

Urging her into bed, he lay beside her, head propped on his arm. "I want to love you, but I don't want this to end." He trailed his finger from the hollow of her throat, between her breasts and down her tummy, then stopped, just above the part of her that wanted him so desperately.

She took his finger and slid it into her mouth, sucking and stroking it with her tongue. Weaving her fingers through his, she said, "We have all afternoon," then placed her hand on his chest and pushed him flat on his back. He grinned as she took the initiative, leaning over him and raining kisses on his neck and all over his chest. With the tip of her tongue, she circled his nipple, then sucked on it.

He took a sharp breath. "Baby, come here." Helping her straddle him, he cupped her breasts, massaging them with his strong fingers.

She threw her head back as her breasts hardened with need. He ran his thumbs over her nipples, and craving shot through her. Clasping her bottom, he pulled her closer, catching her breast in his mouth, suckling and stroking her nipple with his tongue. Her breasts were hot, sensitive, pathways of desire reaching straight to her core. He moved to her other breast, and she sucked in a breath, her mind locked on the sensations his mouth created.

Cash moved her until he was hard beneath her. Holding her hips, he slid her back and forth, the friction sending delicious ripples deep inside her. He pushed her faster, harder. She kissed him, open-mouthed, panting as he worked her body and her mind into a frenzy.

He clasped her shoulders and flipped her over, rising above her, staring down with love and lust shining from his eyes.

She wrapped her legs around his hips. "I love you, Cash."

He leaned in until his mouth was on hers, telling her without words that she was loved. His lips were tender, his hands gentle. As they finally broke apart, he said, "I'll love you forever, Dallas."

Her world shifted. She froze. It had happened. What she'd yearned for, what she'd searched for all her life, was suddenly hers. She had finally found someone she could trust. For the rest of her days. She clutched him to her, understanding fully what she'd nearly lost.

She pushed him onto his back and held him in her hand, stroking him from root to tip.

He inhaled sharply. "Dallas, I don't know—"

She took him in her mouth, and he gasped. "God!"

He clasped her head as she pleasured him with her lips and tongue. This was her gift to him, her way of loving him as perfectly as he loved her.

Cash tensed and yanked her into his arms. "You gotta give me a sec." He kissed her forehead and sighed. "Damn, you're good." Running his fingers through her hair, he asked, "How many kids do you want?"

She grinned. *Boy, does he need to distract himself.* "A couple, at least. How about you?"

"I always figured on three or four. So, we could stick at three, huh? Piper counts as one."

Piper counts as one? Oh my God, I love this man. "Every time I think I can't love you any more, I do."

He squeezed her. "So, how soon can we get married?"

"Uh, soon?"

He tickled her and she squealed, struggling to break his grip.

"How soon?" he asked again.

"I can plan a wedding in maybe...three months?"

He tucked her in under his chin. "I can live with that. And, Dallas?"

"Yeah?"

"I want to pay for it. Your parents aren't able, and I don't want you spending your school money on it."

"Cash—"

"Please, just let me do it. You'll only get married once. Now, enough talking." He rolled her on her back and kneed her legs apart, settling between them. Holding himself above her, grinning devilishly, he said, "Prepare to be loved, woman."

She laughed and pulled him to her, catching his lips in a deep, loving kiss. He was right. Enough talking. Now she wanted to touch and taste and smell the man she loved.

He trailed kisses down her cheek, nibbled her neck, and stopped at the hollow of her throat, tickling her with the tip of his tongue. Goose bumps rose on her arms, and he slid his mouth to her breast, circling her nipple, then flicking it.

She arched into him and he took her in his mouth, the suction drawing aching pleasure from deep inside her. His tongue at her nipple sent flaming shock waves through her. It had been so long since a man had loved her. Yet with Cash, it was more intense, more exquisite.

He took her other breast in his mouth, pushing all else from her mind, until he slid his hand down her belly, cupping her.

Pulse pounding, her core tightened, anticipating his touch.

Leaving her breast, he kissed her greedily and slid his finger between her slippery folds.

She sucked in a breath, arching her hips.

He slid his finger inside her, finding her sensitive spot with his thumb. Kissing her deeply, he thrust with his finger as his thumb rubbed in gentle circles, bringing her to the brink.

Her world became smaller and smaller. It centered around Cash, his strong arms, his hand, his fingers...

He pulled back.

She cried out and opened her eyes.

Grinning at her, he replaced his fingers with his tongue.

Her body gave a surprised jerk. "Oh my God."

"Uh-huh."

Every nerve she had ached for his touch. She raked her fingers through his hair. Her entire body vibrated in response to the sweep of his tongue. A powerful sensation built and throbbed. Heat streaked through her, and she came in quivering waves. She clutched Cash. "Now! Please, now!"

Voice husky, he said, "Come here, baby," and pulled her with him to stand beside the bed. From behind, he grasped her hips. "You okay with this?"

Panting, she said, "Yes, yes."

He touched her back, and she leaned forward. She heard the rip of a condom.

He slid inside her. Though she was wet, he stretched her, and she spread her legs wider. He was all the way in. She felt tight, fuller than ever before. He pulled almost out, then pushed in, quickly this time. She panted, "Yes." Grabbing her hips, he thrust inside her, pulled out and plunged in again, and again. She lost count as he hit her sweet spot with each pounding thrust. She was close, so desperately close to release. She cried out, legs clenching, body convulsing as mindless ecstasy gripped her.

Cash shouted, "I love you," and thrust one, two, three more times, finding his release, clutching her to him.

Legs shaking, she stood, and he wrapped his arms around her. He leaned his cheek on her temple. She turned her face to his and smiled as she kissed him. "I love you more."

Chapter Seventeen

Dallas stood before the mirror in the small dressing room of the church in Howelton where Cash had attended services his whole life. Her wedding dress made her feel like an old-time movie star. She'd chosen a classic A-line design made of tulle lace with a hem that trailed behind her. The off-the-shoulder sleeves and deeply scooped back lent it a graceful elegance.

She clutched her bouquet of pastel roses and shifted nervously in her tall ivory heels as Kate, her maid of honor, adjusted her long lace veil. She hadn't seen Cash in several days and eagerly anticipated being with him in a few short minutes.

Her wedding would be simple but beautiful. The sanctuary was decorated with soft-colored flowers looped together with wide ivory ribbons at each pew and a gorgeous arrangement of pale roses on the table by the pulpit.

Kate hugged her shoulders from behind and met her gaze in the mirror. "You okay?"

She grinned. "Yep. I can't believe I'll be Mrs. Cash Powers when this is all over."

Kissing her cheek, Kate said, "You have fun in Cancún. I had a blast when I was there last year."

Cash's friend Ward Ramsey was feeding the stock for him while they were on their honeymoon. Cash had done the same for Ward when he got married. Dallas was looking forward to getting some rest too. Between working and preparing for the wedding, she was exhausted.

Cash had insisted on something, though. She had turned in her notice at both her jobs, and when they returned from

191

Cancún, for the first time in her life, she'd be a stay-at-home mom. He wanted her to enjoy some downtime before she enrolled at the university.

She stiffened as the organ rang out with the chords of *The Bridal Chorus* from Wagner's opera *Lohengrin*. The lyric, "Here comes the bride," ran through her mind.

Kate covered her face with the veil.

Sarah opened the door, holding Piper's hand. "Come on, girl. Let's go." Sarah led Piper, in her soft pink dress, to her place next to Sarah's son, Colin, the proud ring bearer.

Looking a bit uncomfortable in his tux, Dallas's father came forward and raised his elbow, smiling at her. "Are you ready, honey?"

Kate, beautiful in her pale-yellow gown, stepped in front of them and started their little procession toward the open doors.

Her pulse pounding, Dallas followed. With each step, emotion built in her. Her senses sharpened. The smell of roses grew strong, and, as she entered the sanctuary, her gaze zeroed in on Cash. Her heart leapt. He was breathtaking, like something out of a magazine. His tux fitted his tall, broad-shouldered frame with exquisite perfection. She didn't see the pews filled with his family and friends; didn't acknowledge those who had made the trip to Howelton to wish her well. Instead, her gaze locked with his. Her heart yearned toward him. And, at last, her father led her up the steps to Cash's side.

The pastor asked, "Who gives this woman to be married?"

Her father said, "I do," and passed her hand to Cash.

He squeezed her fingers and grinned at her.

The pastor said, "Stand before me, please."

Cash slipped his arm around her waist and led her to their spot. He held her close as the pastor spoke, explaining their responsibilities to each other and the sanctity of marriage. At last, it was time for their vows.

Jesse, who was best man, handed Cash Dallas's ring.

Holding it to her finger, he began in a clear, strong voice, "I take you, Dallas Royle, for my wife. I promise that my love for you will be an ever-flowing spring. I stand by you, a rock to lean on, a shoulder to cry on, a pillow to rest your head on. I promise you tenderness and undying devotion, promise never to ask you to be more than you are, and to love you for being you. All I have in this world I give to you. I promise to hold and keep you, to comfort, protect, and shelter you, for all the days of my life." He smiled and slid the ring onto her finger.

Her lips parted, and she leaned toward him, tears pooling in her eyes. His words were perfect. She clutched his hand.

He smiled, holding her gaze.

Kate handed Dallas Cash's ring, and she slipped it to his first knuckle, afraid she might drop it if she held it. Still overwhelmed by his words, she swallowed, and said, "I take you, Cash Powers, for my husband. You're the most generous person I've ever known—kind, honest, and loving. I promise to be your hearth, to keep a flame alive for you in my heart. I vow to share my life with you in everything—to respect and love you. I take you to have and to hold, in sickness and in health, not just for this moment, not for an hour, or a day, or a year, but for every season, for every year, forever and ever." She slid the ring onto his finger. He beamed a smile, clasping her hand.

They turned to the pastor as he said, "With the power vested in me, and in the eyes of God and man, I pronounce you husband and wife. You may kiss the bride."

Cash pulled her close, and she trembled in his arms, filled with a joy that surpassed any she'd ever experienced. Gently lifting her veil, he let it fall to her back and teased her lips with a tender kiss, as if to show her how he'd care for her. Then he deepened the kiss, sending a wave of thrills through her body, reminding her of the passion they would have in their marriage. He ended their kiss playfully, with a nip and a smack, grinning as he picked her up and hugged her. He set her on her feet, and the jubilant chords of Mendelssohn's *Wedding March* filled the sanctuary.

He brought her fingers to his lips and kissed them. "I love you, Dallas."

Holding his gaze, she put all the love she had in her voice, "I love you more, Cash." Despite nearly losing him, this perfect man, her ride or die cowboy and the answer to her prayers, was hers at last.

Epilogue

Dallas fought her way through the slow-moving crowd. Even though she was wearing flats, her swollen feet were killing her. Cash would be waiting outside the auditorium, along with his parents and her mom and dad and Piper. They'd all sat together for the ceremony today.

Completing pre-law at Midwestern State in Wichita Falls had been the easy part. Attending law school at Texas A&M in Dallas had been more difficult. Renting a small mobile home on weekdays, she'd driven home to her family every weekend for three long years.

She'd planned on taking Piper with her, but the six-year-old adored Cash, and he had convinced Dallas that he was up to being a full-time dad during the week.

Breaking out into the afternoon sunshine, she walked toward the light pole, their meeting place. As she drew near, she spotted him, standing with her family. Her heart picked up speed, and she rushed the last few feet, throwing herself into his open arms.

He laughed. "Whoa, there, be careful." Kissing her forehead, he set her back down, grinning as the others crowded around her. "You looked gorgeous up there on that stage."

She groaned. "Right, sure I did."

He reached out and rubbed her round, eight-months-pregnant belly. "Most beautiful woman on the planet, and don't argue with me."

God, how she loved this man. They'd waited to plan a family until her last year in school. Now, she'd take time off and enjoy being a momma. When she was ready to start working, she had a job lined up in Howelton with a lifelong friend of Cash's father's. The hometown lawyer wanted someone who would take over his family law practice when he eventually retired.

The baby kicked under Cash's hand, and he grinned. "Easy, buddy, it's just Daddy."

As soon as they'd learned she was carrying a boy, Cash had picked out newborn jeans and a long-sleeved shirt. When he was a little older, her son would have tiny little boots, a belt, and a cowboy hat just like his daddy's.

Cash handed his phone to his father. "Take some pictures. And don't forget how I showed you. We're framing these."

Piper held Dallas's diploma and pressed against her momma as Dallas slipped her arm around her. Cash, on Dallas's other side, put one arm around her and the other hand on her tummy. As he always did, he gave her belly a little pat.

A warm wave of joy swept through her. She leaned her head into him and smiled for the camera.

SNEAK PREVIEW OF HER MIRACLE COWBOY

Acacia Richards finished cleaning Bobby up and fastened his clothing. It had been all she could do to drag herself out of bed this morning, and now she had only minutes until her twin brother's new physical therapist arrived. She lowered him from the bed and settled him into his wheelchair. Morning sunlight shone bright through the open curtains on Bobby's dark-blond hair.

She closed her eyes. *God, I can't do this anymore. Please, I just can't.* Hot tears pooled behind her eyelids. But tears were useless. She'd learned that a long time ago. A moment later, the doorbell rang. Slowly her eyes opened, and she blinked them dry.

Bobby grinned.

The corner of her mouth tilted up, and she wheeled him into the living room, stopping the chair in front of the TV where his cartoons played.

Still wearing the leggings and T-shirt she'd slept in, she hadn't even brushed her hair before wadding it up and clipping it behind her head. She didn't need a mirror to know that the usual circles under her eyes would be dark from lack of sleep. Cursed as she was with a porcelain doll's skin, the slightest blemish showed clearly.

When she opened the door, instant heat crawled toward her cheeks. Instead of a woman like Marilyn, their previous PT, she faced a tall, rocking-hot guy in a scrub top and Wranglers pressed so stiff they'd stand on their own. A crisp, fresh cologne wafted past her nose.

His light-brown eyes twinkled, surely at her dumbstruck expression.

"C-come in. Sorry, I got up late. I mean, we're ready now. But just barely," she stammered, like an idiot. Had Marilyn said her replacement was a man? How had she missed that? His shirt stretched over his chest and upper arms, and his jeans hugged his narrow hips. Acacia couldn't help but stare. His body was raw, sculpted muscle. He was by far the finest male specimen she'd laid eyes on in a while. She took a deep breath and backed away from the door.

He grinned as he entered the room and offered his hand. "Hi, I'm Noah Rowden. If you need more time, please, go ahead."

Her girly brain screamed at her to run for the sanctuary of the bedroom to repair her appearance. Instead, she shook his hand, a tight smile on her face, and walked into the living room. Turning Bobby's wheelchair around, she patted his shoulders. "This is Noah. He'll help you like Marilyn did. Noah, meet my brother, Bobby."

The therapist bent down and shook her brother's hand, saying, "May I give you something?"

Bobby grinned crookedly. "Uh-huh."

Noah wrapped his arms around her brother's broad shoulders and squeezed him in a gentle hug. "That was from Marilyn. She told me what a hard worker you are and said she misses you."

Still smiling, Bobby said, "Marilyn. I love Marilyn," in his slightly slurred voice.

Noah knelt on the floor. "She loves you too." Unzipping his therapy bag, he pulled out a file folder.

Acacia knew what it would say. Her brother had amnesia, the cognitive functioning of a four-year-old, and was quadriplegic. Thank you, Afghanistan.

After making a quick note, Noah returned the folder to his bag and searched inside again, finally bringing out a large red toy car with a raised yellow button on top. "I brought you something to play with."

Her brother laughed, and his arms made small spastic movements while his blue eyes focused on the car.

Noah pushed the button, and a loud siren sound wailed through the room while the headlights flashed on and off.

Her brother threw his head back and shrieked his laughter. "I wa-a-ant it. Can I ha-a-ave it?" High emotion made his speech less clear.

"Of course. I'll teach you how to push the button. You have to work hard. I'll leave it here so you can practice." He placed the car in Bobby's lap and helped him move his forearm to the yellow button. The siren filled the room, and Bobby laughed. No matter how many times he succeeded, he never failed to howl with joy.

After a time, the therapy moved to lower body exercises. With the help of the Hoyer lift, Acacia and Noah lowered her brother to a soft blanket on the carpet. Noah worked Bobby's legs one at a time, increasing his flexibility and using every muscle.

Most of the movements were familiar to Acacia, as she did therapy with her brother every morning on the days he didn't have a PT visit.

Noah's shoulder muscles bunched and released, stretching the fabric of his scrub top as he moved Bobby's legs. His long, supple back arched, and she imagined him naked, hovering above her bare breasts. She snapped her head up. *God!* Where in the hell had that come from?

Hopping off the couch, she strode into the kitchen for another cup of coffee. So it was true. After two years, she was desperate, lusting after the first male trapped in her presence. Leaning on the cabinet, she buried her face in her hands. The emptiness she lived with, day in and day out, overwhelmed her. After several moments, she gathered her courage. She was stronger than this. Strong enough to face this man. To face another day—alone.

Acacia reentered the living room as the session wrapped up, and she helped Noah put her brother in the lift, then back into his wheelchair.

Bobby was once a big man at six feet two inches and two hundred pounds. Now he weighed less with muscle loss but was still quite a handful.

A nurse's aide from the Veterans Affairs Department assisted Acacia with Bobby's bath three days a week. One day each week, she had a VA caregiver who stayed a short time with him while she ran errands and bought groceries. The rest of the time she was alone with him. This brought back the crushing weight she'd awakened with, and a deep sigh escaped her.

Noah raised a brow. "You okay?"

She spun away from him. How could she feel this way? Her brother was so vulnerable—so helpless. What kind of sister was she to dream of escape? Of a new life? A life without this responsibility? Hot blood rose up her neck. What would this man think of her if he knew she yearned to get away from this house—away from the weight that nearly knocked her to her knees on her bad days? She mumbled, "Uh, yeah. I'm fine."

"Acacia?

Still facing away, she said, "The car is a great idea. I can see where, over time, it may help Bobby gain more control over his arms. He certainly loves it. You're the first one to see him as I do—as a little boy who wants to have fun. That's really who he is now."

"I gathered that from the notes in his file. I like to motivate my patients with fun things because so much of what I do is boring or hard work."

She turned back, her face now under control. "Thank you. I'm sure you'll be good for my brother."

Later that morning, after feeding Bobby the breakfast he'd missed, Acacia retreated to the back porch, her safe place, where she had her container garden. The exquisite taste of a sun-ripened tomato, the crisp pop as she crunched into a fresh jalapeno pepper, or cooking with her home-grown herbs were her greatest pleasures.

Some of the morning's tension eased. What had come over her when Noah was here? That sex fantasy was some kind of crazy. The last two grueling years had worn her strong resolve to care for her twin down to a ragged thing. She hardly recognized herself anymore. Physically she was thinner, honed to a strange, harder replica of herself. Emotionally, she was strung out, tuned to a raw edge.

But the worst part, what had become increasingly hard to bear, was the isolation. The four walls of her home had been closing in on her the past few months. The people she was close to were back in Howelton, in North Texas. While caring for her brother, she had no avenue to meet new people, to go out and blow off steam. Bone-deep, she felt the lack of friends, of family surrounding her. Though her best friend, Sarah, came as often as possible, her visits just weren't enough. Way down at the bottom of Acacia's soul there was a big, black nothing where Johnny used to be. Loving him back then, before Bobby, had filled her to the brim.

She missed it terribly. Romance. Having a man's strong arms around her. Adoring everything about Johnny and planning her dream wedding with her friends. This was her darkest secret. How ugly was this need of hers when her poor brother had lost his body, his soul, serving his country? Everything that was Bobby had been blown up on a battlefield in Afghanistan. And little Acacia wanted romance? She couldn't stomach herself sometimes.

After setting her now-empty iced-tea glass down on the table, she grabbed her gardening basket and shears. The spicy smells of her pepper and tomato plants called to her. Pruning and harvesting her vegetable garden was one of her most treasured joys. She chewed her lower lip. Noah had said he'd see her brother on Tuesdays and Thursdays. That gave her two days to get herself under control.

* * *

Noah grabbed a bag of feed from the flatbed trailer and stacked it in the barn. Ronnie, his best friend and roping partner, was right behind him with another sack. They'd just gotten home from Jupe Mills in Fredericksburg, where they'd bought horse and cattle feed at bulk price. The ranch had been in Noah's family for three generations. As the only healthy male heir in the family, he was incredibly lucky to have inherited it.

Ronnie reached out, stopping his friend before he grabbed his next bag. "What about this new client you mentioned?"

"He's a cool guy. An Afghanistan veteran. Came back a mess. His sister's taking care of him. Thing is, he's like a young child now—has severe intellectual disabilities. Acacia, his sister, is wonderful. Been caring for him two years."

"What's she look like? I can see you like her."

Noah took his hat off and squeezed the brim, wiping sweat from his brow. "Well, she's a looker, all right. But she's worn down. Life hasn't been easy on her. Her hair's real dark, and her skin's pale. Looks like you might blow her over with a feather. Makes a man want to take care of her, you know? Something about the eyes." He put on his hat. "She's tough, though. I got that too."

He hadn't been able to quit thinking about her. With her hair pulled back in a simple clip, she had a wholesome, sexy look, though her solemn expression made her seem sad. And her lips—they were just full enough to be tempting without detracting from her overall air of sweetness.

Ronnie raised a brow. "Sounds like you're into her."

Noah headed over to pick up another sack, breathing in a hint of the sweet feed inside. "Not sure what I can do about it, if I am."

Ronnie followed him, not giving up. "Well, you said your client's like a child, right?"

"Yep."

"She could use a man in her life, you ask me."

Noah turned, hands on his hips. "I'm not asking you, all right? I can't do something like that. I'm Bobby's therapist. It wouldn't be right."

Ronnie stood his ground. "I say you can. She's not your client, he is. Two years have passed. Is he getting any better?"

"No."

"There you go. You said she's worn down. She needs support. Anyone would. Look at the responsibility she's taken on. Hell, she needs somebody—something—more than what's she got looking her in the face right now."

Noah picked up a bag of feed and walked into the barn.

Ronnie followed with another sack. "Well?"

Noah shook his head. "Well, dammit, nothing's ever easy."

"Nope."

Noah gusted out a breath. Bobby was part of the problem. He reminded him of Joe. His older brother had suffered a traumatic brain injury when he was five years old while mutton busting at a local rodeo. The sheep he was riding ran him head-on into a steel pipe fence post. Back then, kids didn't wear helmets. After weeks in a coma, Joe had awakened, but he'd never talked, walked, or cared for himself again.

The guilt of being the son who could run, laugh and play had never left Noah. Watching the physical therapists work tirelessly with Joe's lifeless arms and legs had inspired Noah in his vocation. He wanted to make a difference in his patients' lives. And he did. Well, most of the time. But the cases like Joe's, and maybe Bobby's, broke his heart. Many times, his job was holding back the tide of muscle deterioration, not improving a patient's condition.

He had hope for Bobby, though. There was a chance that he might increase his arm control. Noah would give it everything he had for that chance.

KEEP READING FOR A FREE BOOK OFFER!

GET YOUR FREE BOOK

www.janalynknight.com

ALSO BY JANALYN KNIGHT

Cowboy for a Season
True Blue Texas Cowboy
The Govain Cowboys Series
The Cowboy's Fate
The Cowboy's Choice
The Cowboy's Wish
The Howelton Texas Series
Cowboy Refuge
Cowboy Promise
Cowboy Strong
The Tough Texan Series
Stone One Tough Texan
North Their Tough Texan
Clint Her Tough Texan
The Cowboy SEALs Series
The Cowboy SEAL's Secret Baby
The Cowboy SEAL's Daddy School
The Cowboy SEAL'S Second Chance
The Texas Knight Series
Her Guardian Angel Cowboy
Her Ride or Die Cowboy
Her Miracle Cowboy
Find your next handsome hunk now at
Janalyn Knight Books on Amazon[1]

---

1. https://www.amazon.com/Janalyn-Knight/e/
B07RPH8GJ6?ref_=dbs_p_ebk_r00_abau_000000

DEAR READER

Thank you so much for reading my books. Drop by jana-lynknight.com[1] and join my *Wranglers Readers Group* to be the first to get a look at my newest books and to enter my many giveaways. Or, if you like leaving reviews of the books you read, become a member of my POSSE ARC Review Team at my Join my POSSE[2] page and get advance copies of my new books in exchange for leaving honest reviews.

Until next time, may all your dreams be of cowboys!

Janalyn Knight

---

1. https://janalynknight.com/

2. https://janalynknight.com/join-my-posse/

If you enjoyed Cash's and Dallas's book, please leave a review. Reviews are the life's-blood of an author's living and are very much appreciated!

PLEASE REVIEW ON AMAZON

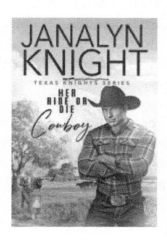

COPYRIGHT

About the Author

Nobody knows sexy Texas cowboys like Janalyn. From an early age, she competed in rodeo, later working on a ten-thousand-acre cattle ranch, and these experiences lend an authenticity to her characters and stories. Janalyn is an avid supporter of the Brighter Days Horse Refuge and totally owns the title of wine drinker extraordinaire. When she's not writing spicy cowboy romances, she's living her dream—sharing her twenty-acres of Texas Hill Country with her daughters and their families.

Read more at https://janalynknight.com/.

Made in the USA
Las Vegas, NV
16 March 2022

45779972R00125